STILL

EDITED BY ROELOF BAKKER

NEGATIVE PRESS
L O N D O N

PHOTOGRAPHS

ROELOF BAKKER

WRITING

RICHARD BEARD

ANDREW BLACKMAN

SJ BUTLER

MYRIAM FREY

SL GREY

TANIA HERSHMAN

JAMES HIGGERSON

JUSTIN HILL

NICHOLAS HOGG

AVA HOMA

AAMER HUSSEIN

NINA KILLHAM

DEBORAH KLAASSEN

SARAH LADIPO MANYIKA

CLAIRE MASSEY

JAN VAN MERSBERGEN

BARBARA MHANGAMI-RUWENDE

JAMES MILLER

MARK PIGGOTT

MARY RECHNER

DAVID ROSE

NICHOLAS ROYLE

PREETA SAMARASAN

JAN WOOLF

EVIE WYLD

XU XI

PUBLISHED BY NEGATIVE PRESS LONDON

29 Rosebery Gardens, London N8 8SH, United Kingdom. www.neg-press.com

First edition 2012

Photographs and introduction © Roelof Bakker 2012

Individual contributions © the contributors 2012

Editor: Roelof Bakker

Design: NEGATIVE Design

Printed in Great Britain by Pureprint

ISBN 978-0-9573828-0-0 paperback

Typeset in Museo 300

NEGATIVE PRESS
L O N D O N

STILL

CONTENTS

INTRODUCTION

THE IDEA FOR THIS book came about when I was looking at ways of putting together a collection of photographs from my art project and exhibition, *Still*.

Still began as a photographic and video exploration of vacated interior spaces at Hornsey Town Hall – a heritage-listed Modernist municipal building in north London that has not been in public use since the 1980s.

For a number of photographs, objects unearthed from storage were placed into new settings, and in the video former functions are re-enacted: drawers slam, lights are switched on and off and the battered out-of-tune piano is played.

A selection of photographs and the video were exhibited inside Hornsey Town Hall itself, allowing the building temporarily to regain a public function, adding a new layer of energy and activity to its history. The exhibition opened on 4 November 2010, the Town Hall's 75th anniversary.

Why not allow the photographs themselves to be re-energised, too, I thought, and set them free from their actual north London location, discovering new meanings along the way?

The idea was born to initiate a creative collaboration in the shape of a literary art book combining photographs from *Still* with new short stories inspired by the images.

As Andrew Blackman, writer of the acclaimed road trip novel *On the Holloway Road* (Legend Press, 2009), had written about the exhibition on his blog, I got in touch with him to see if he would be interested in contributing to a book of this kind. Right from the start, Blackman was excited and generously offered advice. To help kickstart the project, he contacted a number of writers who he thought would find the book's approach interesting.

From that point on, I spent much of my time reading, researching and contacting writers from the UK and abroad. Participating writers were invited to select a photograph that would inspire a piece of new writing. A year and a half later, *Still* is the first print publication from Negative Press London and features new work by twenty-six emerging and established international writers.

What makes this collaborative anthology unique is not only the mix of writers, but also the variety of stories they have written. The photographs all share the same north London location, but the writers allow the images to take on new meanings as they travel through time and space, employing different genres and stylistic approaches.

The aim is that by juxtaposing the stories with the photographs that inspired them, *Still* becomes both an art book and a literary work, as well as a work of art in its own right.

— Roelof Bakker, August 2012

MIDNIGHT HOLLOW

MARK PIGGOTT

C LUTCHING THE BALL OF keys firmly in his hand Edward limped up the dimming high street to the town hall, gasping with fear as if pursued by a ramshackle army of ghosts, woozy from the pints of tan he'd taken in the Shamrock as he attempted to persuade Bert to lend him entry to his past.

Reaching the Victorian building with its mock-turrets, its Georgian facades, its blinded windows, he climbed twenty-three dusty cement steps to the main entrance, wheezing, lungs sore, metal pricking his calloused palms. Reaching the top step he turned and looked out on the high street for the first time since he'd retired: it was almost empty despite the hour, the charity shops closing and pedestrians too scared to linger longer than was necessary to strip the pound shop shelves. The sun gave the rooftops a final yellow lick: turning, he inserted the master.

The main double doors opened onto the once-grand central hall, its wide marble steps curving up round each side, meeting to form a mezzanine then rising together to the first floor chamber where weddings took place. Edward and Dolly had hoped to marry here just as the Sixties began to swing, but the registrar refused to allow it: Dolly had been married before, to a Spanish sailor named Eduardo (Edward hadn't discovered this chilly coincidence till years later) who had disappeared at sea.

In retrospect, their whole married life had been sullied by that seemingly trivial disappointment, Edward's failure as a man laid out for all to see. Dolly's first husband, the mysterious Eduardo (the vowel-combo sounding more akin to Portuguese to Edward's inexpert ear) – whose imperishable youth sneered at him when he checked to make sure Doll still carried his image in her purse – had been a real man, wrestling man-eating octopi and force ten storms. He wouldn't have listened to an ageing registrar with wonky eyes and a buzzing hearing-aid who had ushered them out the door with disapproving tuts that Dolly had impersonated till the second she died, disapproving even still.

Out of habit Edward peeked across to the reception desk, but naturally the building was empty: it was Friday night and the offices, the corridors, the council chambers and lavatories were filled with the ghastly pale sheen of the new neon lights that saved the planet by darkening corners.

Beneath the curving staircase to his left a plain wooden door carried a faded brass plate bearing the unimprovable word 'maintenance'. Edward held up the bunch of keys to one of the long pale lights, squinting, sweating from the Shamrock's poorly piped booze, old barman Stan long gone to the crematorium, his smoke and Dolly's entwined and rising, the place now staffed by Poles who had never tasted real ale in their strange cold towns.

He'd forgotten how many keys there were, each door with its own unique DNA, a different fish-tail for every corridor of lights, the Chubbs and Yales and keys for padlocks long since rusted and discarded in one of the many maintenance cupboards – each with keys of their own.

As he shuffled, squinting, heart banging, Edward thought he heard a faraway noise: a laugh, a cough, perhaps a dog-eared file being slapped on a dusty old desk. He froze: silence, just the sound of buses idling outside, cars revving as if scared even to idle, gangs of kids off to the park to do whatever passed for kicks these days: the same, he reminded himself, as ever was, just with different toys.

Finding the right key he opened the maintenance cupboard door with a loud creak; beyond, a black hole waited to suck him in. Edward slid trembling fingers along the dank inner wall for the light.

Instead of a switch his groping fingers found a round, convex button; how many years since this job had been his? When the interior light appeared – a slow light that seemed to take ages to reach the corners, had man's progress come to this, had he really slowed down light? – Edward jumped. There, in the middle of the caretaker's cluttered cupboard, in a cleared space a few feet square, six or seven broomsticks stood upright, like sentries, like terracotta warriors awaiting the order to march: Edward froze again, motionless as the brooms.

He breathed: until then he hadn't realised he'd been holding his diaphragm. As he exhaled, a bitter old gust from his gut toppled the first broom, which hit another, and all the broomsticks fell down in a haphazard nest, making a clumsy wooden noise that echoed off the heaving shelves overloaded with old boxes of nails, screws, tools and dirty cleaning fluids.

Bert had played a trick: how long had it taken him, giggling like a half-wit, as impatient office workers banged on the door, to stand all the brooms upright? Edward cursed him, that interloper, that opportunist, located the buffing machine behind a battered locker on which were stuck images of deviant love, somehow pulled the floppy metal skeleton out from its hiding place and took a shuddery breath.

As he enticed the unwieldy machine out onto the hard boards of the hall he thought he heard another noise, stopped: nothing. In the store he found the jerry can of cleaning fluid and scratched his head: where did it go? Then he saw the old stone sink full of half-empty paint tins and remembered: a dribble of fluid, then fill the tank with water, just enough to buff one floor. He unravelled the waterproof cord and found a socket, pushed in the plug and flicked the switch: the shaggy wheel slowly turned with that pleasing hum.

Funny how it all came back: when polishing the town hall floors all those years before, he'd found a routine to suit, first a sweep and then the Hoover for dust, two rounds with the buffer, two circuits applying varnish with a brand new mop. But there wasn't time: no time to dust, no time to varnish, only time for one grand sweep of the corridors with the old machine that made soft bubbling noises as the circular disk of wool caressed the wood-effect linoleum.

His route took him along the curved wall and through the door next to the reception desk, along a long, straight corridor lined with closed office doors, each with their darkened squares strafed with wire mesh, through the double-door that led to the modern extension, going back for the plug every few yards like a mountaineer, feeling watched as he passed beneath darkening skylights, the offices all empty and dark with patches on each desk where had stood the computers and assorted ephemerals, sharp right, past the sealed-off annexe where they had found the asbestos and closed the building for three long years (nobody noticed), through another set of doors, then back towards the reception area, timing it just right so he had enough soapy water to wet and clean every inch.

Back at reception he pressed the button for the disabled lift out of habit, but of course it was all shut down so Edward lugged the machine up the curved flight of stairs, metal tubes bashing his shins, panting like he was about to drop, to the mezzanine, where a stern bust of the first borough mayor had stood until some loon from resources said the black marble head was 'too white'.

Something was building, bothering him deeply, but every time he tried to analyse the situation it skipped out of reach round darkened corridors and out, into the unknowable distance beyond.

Edward looked at the huge clock that floated above the lobby but it had stopped – rather, it had *been* stopped. He calculated it had taken two hours to complete the ground floor; two levels to go, each a little shorter than the last. He'd be back in the Shamrock for last orders and then home to the chip pan and an unmade bed. Yet still he felt this unease, as if Dolly was peeking through one of those dark key-holes with derision in her eyes as her dago sailor porked her from behind.

Using the machine as an awkward crutch, he went up to the first floor, plugged it in and went to work. It was odd how often the plug worked loose from its socket, as if some perverse imp was behind him sabotaging his efforts. He kept going back and plugging it in, making footprints in his shining floor: so many footprints, as if he were now being followed by a herd of devilish goats.

By the time he'd completed the second circuit – which seemed much longer than he recalled, longer than the ground floor beneath it, though that was impossible – Edward felt shattered from the physical exertion and his ears throbbed from the incessant bumble of the machine. He had by now quite forgotten why he had begged Bert for the keys; forgotten how many pints it had cost him; even Bert's face was now only a hole.

In the first floor maintenance cupboard he ate a ham sandwich and drank a Coke, mopping his brow with a clean mop and inspecting with interest the rising damp in his old grey trainers.

He'd forgotten how it took it out of you, buffing the floors. Been sat on his arse too long: promoted through the ranks, supervisor to office services manager, even that heady eight months as mayor until they found out about the worksheet discrepancies of Madge, she of the tight pinny and suggestive smiles, who had led him that merry dance through these dark echoing corridors.

The first floor had taken him perhaps four hours: no time now for the Shamrock and its dark Poles, just a frightening walk home along cold pavements, past the shouty flats, up to his room and the bottle he kept for emergencies. He could leave now: who cared about the top floor? The only ones who went there were rats and magpies that nested in old corners; no-one would notice a dusty old floor. If he dropped dead up there they'd never find him.

But that wasn't the way he'd been made: for all his faults.

Sighing, Edward finished his Coke and lugged the clanking buffer up the final flight of stairs. This floor was the smallest and easiest; he could be done in an hour. But even as he plugged in the machine he remembered with a shudder why he'd never liked coming to the top floor on his rounds. He'd hated the night patrol but the scariest time in the building had been early morning, before the cleaners arrived: rushing across the lobby to disable the alarm, making sure there were no burglars on the premises, unlocking every door, still half-asleep and with his dreams on his heels as he flicked all the lights, heart hammering, Doll warm in bed dreaming of the ocean.

All the offices on the top floor opened out onto a central space where in the old days – before there was such a thing as 'harassment', 'sexism' or 'health and safety', the staff met for parties every Christmas. There would be dancing, music, alcohol; things got out of hand. Office affairs, jealousies, resentments, all that simmering sexual and violent tension which had been building all year would burst out like crazy fireworks skipping round the corridors and the polished floor would be slippery with brown ale, tears, and blood; the next day he'd go in and buff away the stains.

Edward polished the outer corridor, every so often glancing to his right through the glass doors to the central hall. He could see people dancing, fighting, making love, beneath a great sparkling ballroom globe whose lights played on naked bodies. He could see a vast, boiling ocean and his own dear Dolly reaching out to save her drowning sailor. He saw Madge, naked beneath her cleaning pinny, performing a lewd dance with mop and bucket. The sun's first light began tinting the edges of the dance floor and still he remained, leaning on his machine and smiling as he watched the wrecking ball come slamming through the ceiling and break up his beloved floor, the walls, and the windows through which he had been peering and which were now dirty and cracked, cobwebs torn; even the spiders had left him.

MY WIFE THE HYENA

NINA KILLHAM

I AM NOT A BAD man. I work every week day until six. I keep a tidy desk and leave it every night devoid of clutter. I have worked my way up to my own office with a window. It overlooks the parking lot where my four-door sedan awaits. Bought with my first and only merit raise.

I am a family man. Of course. With three children whom I suspect I love. And a wife who has a steady part-time job which allows for the occasional trip to our caravan by the sea.

I keep my office door open though no one ever thinks to visit. I don't know why. Busy people with busy lives, I suppose. But every evening I look up from my papers and listen to my colleagues call to each other when they head out to the corner pub.

During the yearly office party, my wife and I stand on the periphery, stiff drinks in hand, alone. My wife, I can feel her tense by my side. She is not like the other wives, who are younger, prettier and usually on the other side of the cavernous room. Because they avoid us, me and my wife. As if she is catching.

Maybe I'm used to it. Her distinctive canine look, her ears twitching, her mouth emitting sharp yaps.

We're all used to it. Our children find it perfectly normal to be held by the scruff of the neck.

Chloe doesn't bat an eye when her mother barrels into her for refusing to do her homework. My wife clutches at her throat with her fangs until my daughter acquiesces. Chloe just brushes herself off, refuses to look her mother in the eye and bounds into the hall to fetch her book bag.

It was unfortunate that my boss was once there to witness the struggle. The one time he agreed to come over for a drink. The man had been helping himself to hummus and pita but his bite remained unchewed in his mouth at the shock.

What are you staring at? Emma – that's my wife – growled as she padded past.

The word must have gotten out because the next morning I saw their smiles, one part sympathy, three parts smirk.

And yes, it's uncomfortable. This is, after all, my office. The place I go to every day. I am in 8:30 sharp and listen as the others stumble in. I see their smiles flashed to each other as I walk past at noon on my way to buy a sandwich. The low Grrrr the head one emits.

They don't see her the way I do.

They don't know that alone in my office, I can't stop thinking of her. Sitting at my desk I find myself dreaming about the way her large tongue hangs dripping when she lies on the bed in a pant. You see, she is everything I want in a wife. Can those men in the other offices say that?

Every night she reads to the twins, letting the two children lean back against her flanks. Jessie likes to hold her tail and stroke it. Emma flicks it away when it gets too rough.

In the meantime, I go to the bathroom to brush my teeth. I take one condom out of the pack and slide it under my pillow. And then watch her come to bed with anticipation.

Most nights she trots in, noses shut the door and opens her large mouth wide in a protracted yawn. Her eyes are rimmed with black, her nose wet and glistening. I lie in bed, covers to my chin and watch her. She jumps up and flops onto the bed and noses her privates, licking and picking. I try to turn my eyes away. But can't get away from the sound of the slurping. I feel aroused.

She always turns three times then flops down, groaning, with her nose on the pillow.

Emma, I'll whisper.

No response. I'll lift my head and look over. And she'll be fast asleep.

Sometimes I'll put my hand on her shoulder and give it a little shake. The low growl is unmistakable. My hand jerks back. And I'll watch as her mottled tongue swings itself over her nose again. She settles back into sleep. The sound of her deep breathing actually calms me. And we'll both slumber deeply, sometimes with my hand on her flank, completely at peace.

Some nights I get lucky.

And today is my birthday.

As I tidy my desk to go home, I think briefly of the usual cards I expect from the children – bought by their mother and scrawled indifferently with their names. I think of the hastily wrapped electrical gadget – invariably the wrong one – from my wife. And the tight, endless call from the great aunt who raised me.

But mainly I think about my birthday treat.

Which is why it's so difficult today to concentrate on work. All day my thoughts have drifted home. I sit here and catch whiffs of her scent.

Her cooking is never memorable. It is difficult to cook with four paws. And tonight will be no exception.

After the store-bought cake is eaten, crumbs licked clean, the children will race away. I will gaze with lager-glazed eyes over the kitchen table to where my wife sits, furry ears pricked, her black liquid eyes bright. I will watch as she laughs, as she does most nights, at me, her spotted haunches shaking with mirth.

Upstairs my children will squabble. But I will look around my kitchen, the kitchen I pay for by sitting in my office every day for the last 15 years, and see my wife's footprints leading from the door, still muddy and wet. I will listen to her pad around the kitchen, nosing closed the dishwasher, her toenails clicking on the linoleum floor. I will follow her up the stairs.

I will wait for her, naked, the sheets up to my chin. And I will think of my empty office and of my dismissive colleagues and of their difficult wives. I've caught glimpses of the tails dragging beneath their dresses. The spots their make-up fails to completely conceal.

These colleagues know it's my birthday. The secretary has pointedly passed along a card for them to sign. I look at their signatures, some big and bold, others small and severely slanted.

Later when the hours draw to a close I can hear them talking, no doubt wondering if they should invite me, just this once. But the head one mumbles something that produces a loud guffaw. I hear them crowd into the elevator together and listen as the doors close.

But it doesn't matter. Really. I would have said no anyway.

It is my birthday and my wife is planning something nice.

I hurry home, leaving their card propped up on my desk.

They act is if I don't exist.

But I do exist. I certainly do.

I am not some joke to be mumbled with a rolled eye, fag in hand and a freshly drawn pint on the table.

Because they know. They know. They've only got to hear their wives laugh, haven't they?

SANCTUARY

ANDREW BLACKMAN

I T WAS AN ODD church in which to claim the ancient right of sanctuary. One of those squat, red-brick churches, too modern to indulge in crosses and spires, the sort that could have been mistaken for a warehouse or a funeral parlour if not for the 'JESUS LOVES YOU' sign outside. When he was first posted to the parish, Reverend Samuels used to change the message every week but, after local vandals had rearranged the letters into obscene anagrams once too often, he superglued the letters to the board and made 'JESUS LOVES YOU' a permanent message to passing commuters on the Kilburn High Road. Some days, he wasn't sure he believed it any more than they did.

'Jesus loves me,' said the man. He had passed the sign many times on his way to work, and perhaps that was why, as he was driving at seventy-five miles per hour down Kilburn High Road with a blood-soaked T-shirt clinging to his oversized belly, he instinctively hit the brakes and lurched into the potholed church carpark.

'Of course. Jesus loves all of us.' Reverend Samuels talked slowly and softly, as if it was the most normal thing in the world for a blood-soaked man to burst into his church demanding sanctuary on a Tuesday afternoon between lunch and evensong. He looked over the man's shoulder as he spoke, fixing his eyes on the Easter display contributed by the Year 1 students at St Saviour's primary school, letting the crude plasticine crosses and lumpy papier-mâché bunnies erase the image of the wild-eyed man with blood congealed on his faded Italia '90 T-shirt and a piece of metal jutting from his hip pocket that could only be the butt of a gun.

'How do you think this is going to end?'

'That's up to Jesus, isn't it, Reverend? I've put myself in his hands.' The man shifted from one foot to the other, looking down at them as if surprised to discover they were shoeless. 'All I'm saying is, if he loves me, he'll look after me, won't he?'

Reverend Samuels kept looking at the Easter display, waiting for guidance, but none came. None ever came. He never knew the right thing to do. A light-headedness washed over him and he wanted to sit down, but forced himself to keep standing, as if by doing so he could keep the man's presence temporary, as if his puny cleric's body could block off the altar and keep him where he was, standing awkwardly at the end of the aisle, near the door.

A mechanised voice broke the silence, announcing that the man had only five minutes left. Ultimatums had come and gone before, but this one felt permanent. Only five minutes left and they hadn't changed it.

'They're coming in this time.'

'Not if you stop them. Tell them this is holy ground, they've got no business here.'

'It's not that simple.'

'It can be. "All authority in heaven and on earth has been given to me." Sounds pretty simple to me.' He jerked his head over his shoulder. 'They have no authority in here.' Still, he couldn't help glancing at the clock, the hand moving with unseen force towards the appointed time.

Reverend Samuels wished he could believe in something so simple and pure. But he was thinking of the police, of their guns and riot gear invading his church, knocking over his Easter display. 'Come on, just put the gun down, give yourself up, and it'll all be over.'

'You're not listening to me...'

Reverend Samuels kept stepping forward, mouthing more calm-voiced promises borrowed from TV cop shows.

'Jesus loves me!' the man shouted, his voice echoing off the bare white walls. 'Just letters on a sign, isn't it? Something to draw people in and make them put money in the collection plate so you can build a new font. No different from "Obey Your Thirst" or "Just Do It".' He looked down at his bare toes splayed on the cold grey tiles. 'I thought it would be different, but it's not.'

Reverend Samuels swallowed, and was surprised how loud it sounded. In spite of everything, he wanted to help this man, this hopeless sinner who was throwing himself on the mercy of the church. His mind desperately scanned Biblical verses for arguments to throw back in the man's face, but came up only with images of blood and sacrifice, washing clean the sins of the world. 'You're being unreasonable,' he said, an edge to his voice, fear and loathing poisoning his words. 'You need to face up to what you've done.'

The man looked at him with disgust, but made his voice slow and quiet. 'I demand sanctuary.'

Just then the ancient bells of nearby St Stephen's began to clank out their tinny quarter-hour chime. The heavy wooden door flew open and smacked against the wall behind with such force that several leaflets on the meaning of life were dislodged from the adjacent desk and fluttered to the ground. Police clad in black flak-jackets fanned out around the church in a move that had clearly been choreographed during the hours of inactivity outside.

The man turned to face them, grabbing Reverend Samuels and pressing the gun to his head. He backed away towards the altar, which, in keeping with the church's minimalist design principles, consisted of no more than a slightly raised platform with a plain wooden table on it. The police were barking orders, but the words echoed off the walls and collided with each other, destroying any meaning they may once have had. The man said nothing in response. He just drew Reverend Samuels closer to him, pressing the gun into his temple.

In the sudden closeness, Reverend Samuels didn't see the police sheltering behind pews or hear the barked orders. He just felt the soft warmth of the man's hand on his neck, the pulse of human blood flooding every finger. The man's sticky breath rippled over his shoulder, carrying with it the trace of his lunch, salami and cheese, laced with the bitterness of coffee. The arm that held him close was covered with dark hair and bore a tattoo of a broken heart. He could feel muscles twitching, fingers pulling nervously at a loose strand of cotton. The man was pulling him closer now, closer than he needed to pull him. It was not protection he wanted but comfort, the simple human comfort that priests have given to dying men for centuries. *Ego te absolvo.*

Seconds passed, or minutes. Eventually the man leaned in closer. 'I know what the ending is now,' he whispered. 'It doesn't involve you. I'm sorry I ever involved you.' He loosened his grip slightly, not enough to be seen by the police, but enough to let Reverend Samuels know he was free. 'I'm going to start shooting. When I say the word, you drop to the ground, okay?' Reverend Samuels nodded, or tried to. He could hear the fear in the man's voice, the need for reassurance, and wished he could tell him that Jesus would watch over him. But he said nothing.

'Now!' the man hissed, and began to raise his gun. 'Now!' he said again, louder this time.

Reverend Samuels, however, did not move. He wasn't sure why, but he was feeling something he hadn't felt for a long time. He knew that he should protect this man, no matter what he had done. He knew it with the certainty of faith, a certainty beyond earthly logic or laws.

Behind him the man hesitated for a moment, then closed his eyes, tensed his index finger against the trigger, and took one last breath. Before he could even fire a shot, though, there was a sharp crack, like the snapping of a pencil, followed by the delicate tinkling of a thousand falling fragments of glass. Reverend Samuels looked up at the hole where a stained-glass window had been. The light dazzled him and he looked away, back and down into the darkness behind him, where the man lay in his Italia '90 T-shirt, eyes and mouth open, a dark hole in his temple, blood spattered against the whitewashed wall behind him and flowing in a stream down over the altar, washing the traces of a thousand empty sermons away into the grate, where they would trickle down into the crypt. He backed away as the black-jacketed police swarmed past him like a column of ants ready to devour the still-warm body of the man whose name he didn't even know. There was nothing he could do. He turned, and walked to the open door though which the light of spring flowed like holy water.

CORRIDOR

EVIE WYLD

WHEN I WAS SMALL, I had a large amount of bad dreams. Being buried alive or surrounded by sharks, old men in empty car parks with long black fingers, a large tree lit in the moonlight, the usual sort of thing that makes a child sit up in bed and scream. To calm me down and to try and keep me out of her bed, my mother told me to imagine my brain was a corridor with rooms on either side of it.

'Think of it,' she'd say, 'the brain is in two halves, and when you want to get rid of bad thoughts, all you have to do is step out of one side of your brain and into the corridor that runs down the middle.' She told me to think of the doors running all the way down, how behind each door is something that can be, if it needs to be, shut away. If you can't get rid of the thought of the coffin lid inches from your face, use the coffin lid as a door and step out into the safe, blank, neutral corridor.

Imagine a corridor, if you can stomach it. Has there ever been a corridor that does not make you uneasy? For me, corridor means school or it means hospital. Perhaps this is the reason why whenever I stepped from a room where a camphor laurel tree was in full bloom in the dark, or a shark's tail grazed the side of my boat, I was always dressed in the uniform of a 1940s nurse. I had on those white rubber squeaking shoes, and I marched down the split of my brain holding a clipboard and a large metal ring of Chubb keys, and not looking at the doors on either side of me.

I was supposed to find a new door to open, one that had good things behind it, swimming and making pastry and the house I would have when I was grown. But I preferred to stay in the corridor, pacing up and down, turning crisply on the rubber-soled ball of my foot. Now and then as I became more sleepy, there'd be a door with a safety glass window at face height and inside the room it would be dark, but you could, if you didn't keep your eyes fixed on the clock at the end of the corridor, make out certain things moving behind the glass. There was no pastry-making going on in those rooms, I knew that.

I would jangle my keys and concentrate on the squeak of my shoes on the floor, I would count my footsteps, count how many times I walked one way and then the other. If I lost concentration, which sometimes happened on the edge of sleep, my nurse self might get curious or bored and she might take her big ring of keys and try one in a lock. All the keys were the right keys and the door would open in front of her and she would step in, carefully closing it behind her, because as distracted as she was, she always knew that it would be a mistake to let anything else into that corridor.

THE STAIRCASE TREATMENT

MYRIAM FREY

THE **HEAVY OAK DOOR** rattles shut behind me, blocking out the sunlight and muting the rush hour din to pink noise. Inside, there's a parched note stuck to it, held in place by browned, glassy Sellotape. It reminds the tenants to always lock up after themselves, but no one seems to have bothered. There's a greasy sheen to the square clinker floor tiles and the walls, especially the corners, have a faint sooty patina. I automatically reach for the light switch and the ceiling lamps come on with a click.

I start to walk up the stairs: A B C D E. I pause on the F step to run a finger over the cold wall.

I used to carry you up and down these stairs for hours at a time. Your small white limbs would dangle from the blue corduroy BabyBjörn carrier, the cool air radiating from the walls of the staircase the only thing that ever had a discernible effect on your condition. Inside our flat you were unable to go to sleep; the itch was always worst in the evenings. The rash appeared mainly on your fingers, palms, toes and on the soles of your feet. It wasn't even a rash, really, but nests of tiny round translucent blisters, which turned into perfectly concave pits when scratched open and immediately filled with blood after the serum had leaked out.

After I had you I forgot a lot of words. The midwife said it's quite common and that I shouldn't worry. I was supposed to get back to work after eight weeks, but I couldn't. I particularly struggled with the names of items that contain things, like jar, wallet, oven or school bag (to this day, my brain wants to call the letterbox a fridge). There is no time to search for words in simultaneous translation. No time at all.

The first few weeks after we had found out about the staircase treatment I would just slowly walk around on the landing in front of the flat. You rarely fell asleep in less than an hour, subjecting me to an erosive mixture of stress and utter boredom. My thoughts would go in circles along with my feet and got darker with each round. Eventually, I walked down the two storeys to the ground floor and up again, hoping that the physical activity would make the wait less agonising. It proved too much motion in too short a period, but you seemed to enjoy it. It is impossible to anticipate just how much discipline it requires to walk down a flight of stairs very slowly – muscle memory dictates otherwise. To trick my legs, I invented the alphabetical stair game.

I would pick topics, easy ones at first, and force myself to find words for them in alphabetical order with every step I took. I was not allowed to move on before I knew the word. Initially, I would name trees (ash, beech, chestnut, dogwood), French towns (Evians Les Bains, Fraisse, Grenoble, Honfleur) and kitchen utensils (ice crusher, juicer, knife, lemon zester). As time wore on, I searched for German palindromes (Marktkram, *nennen*, Otto, Pep), anatomical terms (quadriceps, retina, scrotum, thorax) or word pairs with one half deriving from Greek or Latin (urge incontinence, vacuum gauge, water orchid, xerographic printer). Q and X were always a bit of a problem, of course – I allowed myself to skip them on occasion. K didn't always work in English and almost never in French, while C tended to be difficult in German. I had to make certain concessions, but I rarely broke the rules.

There were days when I didn't have the nerve to come up with anything extraordinary and just went through a well-rehearsed downstairs: fruit/upstairs: vegetables routine. When I felt reason to punish myself I would choose an excessively difficult topic, like historic battle sites and wouldn't stop until I was through to Z, even when you had fallen asleep. On a happy day I would amuse myself with quirky alphabets, such as unlikely tattoo motifs that fit on a thigh.

By the time you started primary school I was ready to work again. I accepted a part-time position with the government, even though the commute to the capital was impossibly long. When you were 18, the United Nations offered full-time employment. I moved out and your mates moved in on the same day. We regularly saw each other at weekends;

you even made some friends in Geneva. I was transferred to Strasbourg after two years and then to the UN headquarters and all of a sudden there was this ocean between us that neither could afford to cross very often. Our meetings became less frequent, and so did our phone calls, until we barely communicated beyond the obligatory birthday and Christmas cards. You've turned to using those Hallmark online ones recently. I know your mates found their own lives and flats after you all got your degrees and I'm aware there's a girl who moved in with you somewhat later. I know her name, but I've never seen her. I have no idea how serious things are between the two of you.

Just before I reach the landing I pause again before I go on to ring the doorbell. The lights in the staircase have timed out and die with another click. Before I get to the door it opens and a woman in her twenties emerges. She has long and straight brown hair and wears a pullover with broad blue and white horizontal stripes over black leggings. She unhooks something from the coat stand and straps it around her waist. It's a BabyBjörn carrier. I use the time it takes her to go inside and fetch the child to turn around and walk down the stairs as fast as I can without making too much noise. On the M step I start to cry.

PA-DANG

JAN VAN MERSBERGEN

T HE FIRST THING ANTON asks when I come to pick him up is: Do you have a newspaper with you?

A newspaper?

Yes, a paper. They didn't bring mine this morning.

No, I haven't got one.

Anton says: I think someone stole it.

I say: Anton, I thought you stopped reading the newspapers.

No.

When did you start reading them again?

A while ago.

Poor Anton. He still was collecting horrifying stories. I remember him reading them out loud at home. The look on his face, the glance in his eyes, and his mother pretending not to hear it.

So you really don't have a paper? Not even in the car?

No, not even in the car.

He puts his cigarette in the ashtray, pushes forward a little on the seat of the chair and grabs his cup from the table. We are in the coffee room. In the corner is a TV, high on the wall, showing a music video. The sound is off.

Is the coffee cool enough yet? I ask.

He shakes his head.

You've got to blow.

He picks the cup from the table, puts all his fingers around the cup and brings it close to his mouth. He blows.

Did you sleep well last night? I ask.

What?

I asked whether you slept well.

Yes, says Anton.

Have you got all your stuff packed?

My bag? It's in my room.

Why don't you go and get it? Then we can go.

First my coffee.

Go and get your bag and your coffee will have cooled down by the time you're back.

No, I want my coffee first.

He blows into the cup and then gently takes a sip of coffee.

Good?

Yeah, nice.

It's from a machine, I say.

What?

You like that plastic stuff?

Yep, I like it.

Come on, I say. Time to go.

Anton stays in his seat and takes a sip of coffee. I get up and say: Just bring your coffee with you in the car.

It'll spill.

The cup isn't that full.

He takes a few sips of coffee.

We should go. Will you get your bag?

Anton walks down the corridor to his room, holding his cup. He returns with his bag, but no cup, and we walk together towards the exit. I point to where my car is. We get in and drive to the motorway. The bag is between Anton's feet. His hands on his thighs. We drive along the canal, around a roundabout, through the centre of town and follow the road north.

Who's going to be there? he asks.

Everyone.

Anton looks at the first houses after the roundabout. We pass a big farm. In the field next to the warehouse are a few large machines, yellow and orange.

Is this where it happened? With that man and his leg?

Yes, I say, It was here.

Anton says: He got stuck in a thresher, didn't he?

Yeah, I think so.

Anton smiles. That's the way it went, he says. And nobody helped him. He shouted to the others when he got stuck. He was always playing tricks on them, stupid jokes and that, so nobody went to help him. They thought it was another of his jokes, right? So they just carried on eating their lunch. Is that what you heard, That's right, isn't it?

Yes, I say.

It was lunchtime and they were just eating their sandwiches. And the man was shouting for help.

Anton looks over his shoulder at the machinery next to the warehouse.

Lost his leg, from there down, he says, making a chopping movement on his thigh.

He chuckles.

Because he was always joking around.

We arrive at the house. I park the car and say: Uncle Frans is already here, you see?

That's his car, right?

Yes, the blue one.

What kind of pie has Mum made? he asks.

Apple pie, of course.

I want mine with whipped cream.

Thought you might.

His mother opens the front door and says hi. Uncle Frans is sitting on the couch, a plate with a piece of apple pie on the table in front of him. He says hello to Anton and shakes his hand.

Happy birthday, he says.

Thanks, the boy says.

Twenty-three, but still a boy.

Anton's sister comes out of the kitchen. She kisses him three times, Dutch-style, and wishes him a happy birthday. Hope you'll still be my boy even when you're very, very old, she says.

Yes, says Anton again.

He sits down.

His sister asks him: Do you want coffee and cake?

A piece of apple pie, please, Anton says. With cream. And do you have a newspaper?

What?

You got today's paper?

In the bucket.

Anton stands up and walks to the couch. He walks very slowly. Next to the couch is a wooden bucket with a large handle. He pulls out a few magazines and a newspaper.

Is this today's?

I think so, says his sister.

Why do you need a newspaper, Anton? asks his uncle.

I just need one.

You'd better eat your cake, Uncle Frans says.

Apple pie, says Anton. With cream.

He sits back down. His sister fetches the pie. The forks are on the table, she says.

Anton takes a fork, looks at it, then takes another one. He holds the plate in his other hand, close to his chest.

Problem with the fork? Uncle Frans says.

What? Anton says.

That fork. The other one. Was the other fork no good?.

No, says Anton.

But, they're all the same, Uncle Frans says.

I hate it when Uncle Frans picks on Anton.

Anton picks up another fork. This one is ok, he says.

So, and how are you? asks Uncle Frans. Do you like your new home?

I'm fine, Anton says.

He sticks his fork in a large piece of pie. He eats. Then he picks up the rest of the pie with one hand and collects the crumbs on the saucer with the other hand, with just one finger. He eats like a child.

He says: Here it is.

He's looking at the paper. I can see how hard he's concentrating. Then he says: This Sunday, an unknown man shot a policeman in a house in Princess Beatrix Street.

Is that right?, says Uncle Frans.

Yes, says Anton. The police released the news on Monday. In Princess Beatrix Street.

His uncle drinks his coffee, puts his cup on the saucer and when Anton's mother comes back into the room, with her hair freshly combed, he says: I thought they'd help him, in that madhouse.

They are, says his mother.

He's still into that nonsense, says uncle Frans, and to Anton he adds: So it's going to be just like last year? Like your last birthday.

Anton nods.

That's the point for me to say: Keep your mouth shut, Frans.

Uncle Frans smiles at me.

And you're still the same, too, he says to me in a soft voice.

So are you, I say.

Frans' sister sits down next to Anton on a wooden chair and says: That's OK, Anton.

Yes, says Anton. Do you remember what happened last year, in another small town?

I remember, says Uncle Frans.

A shooting occurred last Tuesday in full view of a number of people who were sitting outside a bar, says Anton in a deep voice.

I listen to his newsreader-voice, an old newsflash.

Anton continues: Four men ended up in hospital with gunshot wounds.

Jesus, Anton, said Uncle Frans.

Anton is quiet. He just looks at his uncle, with his eyes big.

Jesus, says Uncle Frans again.

Anton does not respond for a while. Then he talks slowly, enunciating every syllable:

The shooting occurred at 5pm in Padang Street.

Well, Anton. You sound quite happy about it.

Anton nods. In Padang Street, he said. *Pa-dang!*

He holds out his hand, his thumb up, his index finger forward, the other fingers curled into his palm.

Pa-dang, he says. Get it?

A ROSE FOR RAHA

AVA HOMA

THE LASHES HAVE DRAWN maps on Baba's back and neck. He steps out of the bathroom, a beige towel covering his lower body, and walks upstairs to his room. Every time I see his scars, I feel a furtive stab pierce my back. We look into each other's eyes but we never talk about the lines cut into our father's back and neck. Baba returns to the living room in his baggy grey Kurdish pants and a dark brown shirt. His face and movements are as stern as ever: father is angry with the entire world. My nostrils are filled with the chamomile soap that hides the otherwise strong scent of his body. Placing a pillow under his head, he lies down on the handmade Kurdish rug, a souvenir of his mother; stout and solid, the rug is made of symmetrical knotting of crimson, white, and blue thread over a woollen foundation. Baba covers his eyes with his hairy right arm and his veins stand out. We know we're not supposed to make noise when it's Baba's nap time.

I run to the front yard and you follow me. I am your sister and I am three years older than you and, therefore, your boss. The rose bushes are glowing. You and I pick a yellow one and giggle at our little act of defiance.

'Hey, Farzad, I have a brilliant idea!' I say. 'Let's water the roses so they give us more flowers.'

You obediently run to fetch me the water hose. Your chubby legs, arms and cheeks shake when you run. I agree aloud with what everyone else says: 'You are biteable.'

'Biting's baaaaad,' you say with a frown.

I grab the hose and, to reward your cuteness, start telling you a story. 'Once upon a time, there was a king who said to his son: "You should go kill your sister. She is a bad girl."'

'She is a bad girl, Raha?' You tilt your head and repeat my words with a rising intonation.

'No. The vizier told the girl, "You have to lie with me or I will come up with a plan that will make your father cut your head off."'

'Whhhhhhy?'

'Well, the girl was beautiful and the vizier wanted her.'

'Why didn't she lie with 'im?'

'Because she was a good girl, idiot.'

Your hazelnut eyes look puzzled but you don't ask any more questions. I am too lazy to recite all the details of the story and I don't want the girl in my version to go through so many tests before she can prove her innocence; but I still want her to meet the prince.

'Hmmmm, let's see…' I put the yellow rose in my hair and wonder if I look like a princess now. 'So, the daughter told her father, "I will let you kill me, but you should listen to me first." And then… in something like a courtroom she defeated the vizier bravely and the prince who was there, as a journalist, fell in love with her.' I look at your confused eyes and start laughing at your face and at the idea of a prince as a journalist. You laugh your sweet laugh. I run around the yard and you run after me. This continues for a long time and every time I look back at you, we burst into laughter again.

When we are at daycare, every chance I get, I peek into your classroom to make sure you're happy and no one is picking on you. If they do, I'll hit them. All the kids know this.

'Don't soak those flowers, you idiot!' Baba yells at me when he passes the yard.

I dare not respond.

'We're watering the yellow roses for them to give us more yellow roses,' you explain.

'You're drowning them.' Baba turns off the tap in the middle of the yard where the hose is installed.

I want to say 'At least we don't forget about them,' but my fear stops me.

Baba walks towards me and takes the rose out of my hair. 'Didn't I tell you not to pick the flowers? The landlord will throw us out,' he says and throws the rose away in the garden. Then he looks up to see if the landlord is watching.

You stare at me, waiting for an explanation. Baba shuts the door and I don't cry. Instead, I jump on my bicycle, ride it around the yard as fast as I can and scream for no reason. Hundreds of times, I bike around the water faucet in the middle of the small yard and you bike after me.

'You are the police and I am the thief,' I say.

You and I do not feel nausea, do not need to take a rest in the afternoon, have no schedule, no debt, no grudges.

You come close to arresting me a few times but I do not let you. You are the sweating and out-of-breath police; I am the older, uncatchable criminal. Your beautiful hazelnut eyes – because of them everybody calls you *Chawshin* and loves you more – turn teary when you give up on me in the evening. That is when you go inside the house, turn on the heater, and put your forehead near it. I find some most-likely-expired yoghurt in the fridge, mix it with sugar and eat it with bread to stop my nagging stomach. Baba is never back earlier than ten at night and Mama is back around eight from work.

'*Chawshin gian!*' She puts a hand on your forehead and hugs you.

You are her *Chawshin gian*, the darling with beautiful eyes. I am nobody. 'Farzad's fever is fake,' I declare. I want to tell her you have had your head near the heater to draw her attention. She scolds me for the drops of yoghurt on the kitchen floor. I tell her again you do not have a fever. She touches your forehead and says I am the reason you have a fever, that I am a bad sister and cannot take care of you, that she cannot trust me with anything. I am still hungry. Mama is tired, she sleeps. We go to the fridge; it is empty.

Father cannot find a job despite his PhD in communications and other qualifications. Who'd hire a refugee whose case has not been accepted in three years? Mama has to provide for the family and cannot do the housework. They both say I am big now that I go to middle school, so the housework becomes my responsibility. I have no say in it. I know how to clean but cannot cook. Even so, I cannot clean an entire house by myself and go to school too. Our house is in the poorest neighbourhood, very far from the centre of the town. It's rundown now, without ever having been completely built. The staircase has no railing and the bricks have not been covered by cement. We have one room in the basement, two on the main floor and one in the attic.

Mama and Baba fight over who should pay for the shelves that were bought to make the house a bit tidier, a house that nobody has time for. Shelves aren't any help: dirty laundry is scattered on the floor, the garbage smells in the kitchen, the walls that used to be white are now grey.

I hold your hands and want to take you to Baba's room, upstairs in the attic, where we might not hear them any more. But I am too frightened. Baba gets angry beyond control sometimes, and Mama's room is too cluttered. Our own room is better.

'I swear I'll set the shelves on fire if you don't pay!' Baba roars. 'You promised!'

I hold my palms over your ears.

'Don't you understand, you bastard? I said I don't have money,' Mama shouts.

You stare at me. I know my hands have not blocked the sounds.

'Why did you promise, then? They'll take me to jail if I don't pay tomorrow.'

'So much the better! You and your useless P.h.Shit! You grew up in a barn. Your mother was a whore,' Mama screams. I know she has said the worst thing one can say to Baba.

The floor is shaking. Mama runs and Baba chases after her. I am panicking but want you to stay calm. I find a headset and put it on your ears with shaking hands, attach it to the old, black, dusty radio and turn it on. You look at me, puzzled. I turn up the volume.

'Let go of my hair, you motherfucker!' Mama screams very loudly.

I hold my hands over my ears and press tightly. You laugh. I am not sure if there is something funny on the radio or if it is my face you laugh at. Doors crash and I laugh with you. Your laugh is cute; everyone says so. In the red-and-white striped shirt and pants, you look adorable. My laughs are loud and ugly, but my mouth does not look big to you so I laugh freely around you. Your hard laughter makes you look even more lovable; oh, you're so biteable. When I pinch your chubby red cheeks, I realise your temperature is too high. I know you have not had your head near the heater. Tears form in your eyes and I bite my lips. I have been violent and inappropriate again.

I put two index fingers in the corners of my big mouth and draw them wide, squint my eyes and stick out my tongue. You laugh while your tears roll down. I kiss your tears, crawl on all fours, and tell you to hold the radio in your small hands and jump on my back. Baba roars with anger, Mama shrieks with hate and contempt; I bark for you and crawl around. The headset is on your ears. You laugh.

After I am tired of riding you and you of laughing, we fall asleep. When I wake up, a dried yellow rose is on my pillow.

THE BLIND MAN

NICHOLAS ROYLE

SIMISTER
POLEFIELD
PRESTWICH

AS A YOUNG WOMAN you took the trolleybus to work. Down Moston Lane it went, heading south, and when it turned left to go towards Collyhurst, the trolley would sometimes come off the wire. On those occasions you would be late for work and you would go in and you would say, 'The trolley came off the wire.' No one minded; everyone understood. The trolley came off the wire.

When you were saving up to marry my dad, you would walk the three miles instead. It took you just under an hour. You were a fast walker. You were never late for work then.

Once married, you and my dad moved to another part of the city and you caught the bus into town.

BAGULEY
MOSS SIDE
MANCHESTER

My dad didn't like you working, so you gave up the job. It was no hardship. You liked being at home. When I was a toddler, you would take me places on the bus. You used to leave the pushchair behind the stop. It was always there when we got back.

LANGLEY ROAD
PENDLETON
WEASTE

My dad worked long shifts at the docks. He expected his tea on the table when he got home. He got it, too. I discovered that I could alter the shape

of the lines on his face by how loudly I cried for my tea. I knew that I
created those lines and I could see they were directed not at me but at you.

ECCLES
PEEL GREEN
TRAFFORD PARK

I was ten when I started using the buses by myself and twelve when I began
taking down their numbers and underlining them in a little orange book –
Fleetbook 1: Buses of Greater Manchester. You could get other *Fleetbooks* in
the Ian Allan shop on Piccadilly ramp. *Fleetbook 3: Buses of West Yorkshire,*
which was turquoise. *Fleetbook 7: Buses of the East Midlands* – a drab green.
Fleetbook 15: Buses of Greater London – grey, though I always thought it
should have been red, because the Manchester one was orange, like our
buses. But I couldn't afford them, the *Fleetbooks.* Not on my spends.

SWINTON
MONTON
ECCLES

I used to hear you and my dad rowing downstairs. You kept the door
shut, but the sound came through the floorboards. I bent over my lists of
numbers, looking for the buses I still needed, seeing which garages they
were based at. I would fantasise about visiting them all. I wouldn't stop at
Princess Road and Queens Road and Northenden. I would take the 400 to
Rochdale and Oldham and Stockport. I would jump on the 263 or 264 to
Altrincham.

It was from Altrincham garage that I took the blinds. They didn't let
you go round the garages. It wasn't safe. So you had to creep in. I wrote
down the numbers, breathed in the smell of diesel. I boarded the scrapped
vehicles in the yard at the back. I unscrewed a bell-push. I helped myself

to a square plastic information plate detailing the vehicle's dimensions. The metal trapdoor giving access to the space for the destination blind was normally held in place by two catches: one of them was undone. I forced the other. The blind was easy to remove. I liberated a couple more from two tired old Crossleys and ended up having to run from the yard, a driver's angry cries ringing in my ears.

I hid the blinds at the back of my cupboard and I would take them out when there was no one else in the house and unroll them across the floor. I would read the names of places, some I had been to, others I would never see.

STALYBRIDGE
REDDISH
STOCKPORT

Somehow, you and my dad never came across the blinds, but my dad found the *Fleetbooks* in the hole in the wall I had made behind my desk. It was not quite a full set. I still needed *Fleetbook 13: Buses of Eastern Scotland*. They had never had it in stock at Ian Allan's when I had shoplifted the others, over a period of months.

Did you steal these?

No.

Are you a dirty little shoplifter?

No.

Did you steal them?

No.

Then why were they hidden in a hole behind your desk? A hole in the wall you vandalised for the purpose of hiding your dirty stolen goods. Tell the truth now, tell the truth and we'll forget all about it. The worst thing by far is lying about it. Tell the truth and you'll be forgiven. Did you steal them?

I looked at my dad. I saw you come up behind him, having been interrupted in your housework, a bottle of toilet cleaner in your hand. I couldn't read the expression on your face.

Yes, I said. I stole them.

You dirty little thieving bastard. You dirty little thief.

He took a step towards me, his face red, nostrils flaring. I saw him draw back his hand and I flinched. But, with his hand raised, he turned away from me and pointed a finger in your face. What did he mean? That it was your fault? That you would pay for it later? I never saw him hit you, but there was a violence in him.

You stepped into the space he had vacated and now your face resembled his. Your arm came up in a sudden movement. Either you squeezed the plastic bottle or momentum brought the blue liquid sloshing out of the spout, and the world became a blue film that quickly faded to black.

BELLE VUE

AUDENSHAW

NORTH MANCHESTER GENERAL HOSPITAL

My dad burned the *Fleetbooks*, but I kept the blinds, carrying them from one foster home to another, where they stayed rolled up for most of the time. In the middle of the night – it was all the same to me – I would get them out and unroll them and run my fingers over the smooth canvas, believing I could still read the white letters against the black. And when I finally got my own place, I hung them on the walls. It made the room darker, but that didn't matter to me. I would invite people round and ask them to read them to me.

RADCLIFFE

BESSES O' TH' BARN

PENDLEBURY

Finally, I invited you. I assured you that if I had been angry, I was no longer. You can't remain angry for ever. You came. I invited you in and you entered and sat down. Like any visitor, you were asked if you would read to me from the walls.

SALE MOOR
BROOKLANDS
SOUTHERN CEMETERY

FROM THE ARCHIVE

JAMES MILLER

O F ALL THE ARTEFACTS in the archive, exhibit KODAK 400NC-3 is among the most significant – and also the most puzzling. Here at the Ancient Cultures Research Centre (✿) we understand the image to signify the centrality of the number three[1] (o.o.o.) in Western European society up to the end of the First Digital Age (FDA, 2000-2037).[2] We believe the picture is particularly important as it reveals the role of this number in structuring primitive concepts of authority and justice.

Attention is first drawn to the three white globes set equally above the chair/throne in the image-centre. In the Judeo-Christian religion – a declining but still significant value system during this period – three represents the Godhead: the Father (God himself); the Holy Ghost (the Word or essence of God) and the Son (the corporeal embodiment of God).[3] The Holy Family (itself an idealisation of the Father/Mother/Child family unit that was common practice up to the end of the FDA) were three (Virgin Mary, Joseph and 'baby' Jesus) as were the Wise Men who visited the Son when he was born.[4] The imaginary Christian afterlife of Hell, Purgatory and Heaven as explained in the Holy Books of Milton and Dante is also threefold.[5] The Christian triumvirate has a parallel in the Hindu belief system, which largely replaced the 'religions of the book' following the fall of the FDA.[6] A cosmology of three is replicated in the Hindu Trimurti: Brahma the Creator, Shiva the Destroyer and HSBC the Credit Provider.[7] In the Jedi religion threes are replicated in various forms, particularly with 'Yoda' the wise green man, 'Darth Vader' the dark King and his chosen son 'Luke Skywalker.' Each figure represents a different manifestation of authority, truth and power.[8] Three also had significance in the other major religions from this period, including Islam and Judaism.[9] Although these religions were in almost constant conflict during the FDA, scholars have suggested these numerical structures indicate resonant archetypes within man and reveal enduring continuities of 'human nature' from the archaic epoch of the ancient and Golden world up to the collapse of the FDA.[10]

For our purposes, this artefact is particularly revealing in that it shows how the structuring effects of the number three have shifted from a cosmological or mythological function to a political-judicial function, thus affixing transcendental signification to the otherwise fallible human legislation of the Law. Reading the picture, we clearly see that the three globes form the base of an inverse triangle with the throne placed at the point where symbolic power is concentrated. Further scans of the image show numerous triangle formations within the composition, suggesting a deep architectonic of triplicate meaning in order to stabilise moments of rupture within the semiotics of the Law. We believe the judicial-legislative functions of the state suffered greatly from ambiguity during the FDA and that triplicate, tripartite and triangle formations were used to fix otherwise unstable systems of signification.

Triangle and pyramid formations recur throughout Earth civilisations. The Ancient Cultures Research Centre (✿) has found evidence of vast stone pyramid structures that pre-date the FDA by many thousands of years. These structures exist on different continents and were produced by different cultures. The best-preserved example is in the western deserts of the former United States, a dominant Digital Age culture particularly in thrall to pyramid systems. The pyramids of the United States were built in an area known as 'Last Vegas' – a zone of temples dedicated to the worship and waste of money where vast sums were squandered on games of chance. The pyramid influence is also shown on the currency of the former United States – the dollar – which is distinguished by an image of a pyramid and an eye.[11] The meaning of this symbol has long perplexed historians and archaeologists, but the latest research suggests a connection to what was known as a 'Ponzi scheme'[12] as designed by the notorious Madoff Gang.[13] Although The Ancient Cultures Research Centre (✿) has yet to understand exactly how such schemes functioned, evidence suggests the 'Ponzi' was connected to other economic structures of the period (see also 'Credit Default Swap' and 'Trickle Down')[14] all of which functioned according to a Pyramid formation. Such formations played a crucial part in organising the 'capitalist' mode of production – the dominant economic system up to the end of the FDA. The exact workings of this system were highly irrational and appear largely incomprehensible despite the best efforts of our researchers.[15]

In terms of this artefact, it is our view that the effect of the inverse triangle concentrates power and authority on whoever sat in the central throne, thus giving their role a greater legitimacy and sovereignty within the symbolic economy of this culture. However, other features in the scene continue to perplex. What, for example, of the two chain-like objects that hang between the white globes? Although their position is proportionate and corresponds with parallel structural lines around the throne to indicate further the special value of whoever would have taken that seat, the exact function of these objects is opaque. Further ideologies of symmetry are upset by the fact that the left-side chain appears proportionately longer than the other. Concepts of 'left' and 'right' were quite different in the period up to the end of the FDA, connected to a dense web of now discredited political formations, as well as the physical layout of certain political spaces.[16] Whether the two chains are part of this semiotic system remains ambiguous. Researchers from the Post-Human Institute (■□) + (ʲ) have suggested the chains have a purely functional/technical role, possibly working in tandem with the three white globes or functioning as controllers of the entire scene, able to move walls and seats, alter lighting effects and change the ambient tones and textures.[17]

Great interest has been generated by the round device just above the throne in the middle of the picture – the immediate focus for the viewer's eyes. Most experts agree that this device was a sort of primitive chronometer – a popular means of ordering the day-to-day during this period.[18] Commonly known as a 'clock', these chronometers have been found in a variety of sizes, shapes and locations and were believed to exist as portable, personal ordering devices, as objects of domestic pleasure (often with a unifying function in the key room of a domestic space) and in monumental forms as the centrepiece for symbolic buildings or in the middle of a town, settlement or institution.[19] The role of the chronometer, above the throne and in the centre of the triangle, demonstrates the extent to which a man-managed ordering of the planetary cycle was instrumental in legitimating executive functions.

The chronometer is frozen a little after seven, although which part of the day fell under this symbolic regime is unknown. This time could have referred to either the rising or the setting of the sun or possibly to some indeterminate period between sunrise and sunset. Some scholars have persuasively argued it refers to both.[20] There has been speculation that the indicated time actually refers to the collapse of the FDA, known, in some remnant texts as 'the time-time stood still' or even 'the endtimes.'[21] Archaeologists have tried to identify the moment when the electronic and virtual systems that defined the FDA finally overloaded. It remains a source of some dispute whether there was a single moment of catastrophic collapse or a series of disconnections, breakages and freezings. Following the eventual schism between the real and digital realms, much of civilisation was then excluded from vast reserves of information. Efforts to regain access to this lost information continue, as do moments of leakage and slippage between our world and the lost virtual realm of the FDA.

What image KODAK 400NC-3 actually represents remains unknown. By analysing the numerical symmetries and codes within the image, the Ancient Cultures Research Centre (✿) thinks it likely that the scene represents a seat of power. Whether it is the throne of a King, Prime Minister, President, Grand Mufti, Head Master or some other, lesser executive function is uncertain. The Ancient Cultures Research Centre (✿) asserts that the function of the throne is bound with legalistic and judicial forms of authority. Possibly the throne was intended for one vested with the ability to punish others for the transgression of social codes. The absence of a figure for the throne is also significant. Again, the lack of the sovereign authority in this image cannot be deliberate. We know that towards the end of the FDA there was a great crisis of legitimacy in the signifying systems intended to safeguard meaning. The absence of the sovereign power in this instance is taken as indicative of the wider crisis: where we should find the embodiment of the Law there is only absence, an empty seat. God is dead or at the very least stuck in traffic. We believe that the preponderance of symbolic architecture in the scene demonstrates the inherent insecurity of executive and judicial functions during this period and the concomitant need to overcompensate with an over-coding of power paradigms designed to fix meaning and determine identity.

For further discussions of the archive, please touch **NEXT** to continue.

END NOTES

1   Three was also represented as: 3; Ⅲ; iii; 111; "; ᴦ; γ; 三, 弍 and 叁 depending on particular culture-specific linguistic-cultural registers and semiotic codes.

2   According to the Judeo-Christian calendar system this image dates from the late 20th/early 21st century. See also *First Industrial Age* and *First Media Age*, *History of Ancient Earth Cultures* (New Kong: University of New Kong Press), 3rd edition, eds. Xao Phu et al. #code-ref: ƆCЁÐ#515

3   See Dong Phuzd, *Rituals and Religions of Ancient Earth* (Xian: University of Xian Press), 2nd ed. #code-ref: ᖆ#ǽH_1117777

4   Fragments of various Judeo-Christian scriptures, known collectively as *The Bible*, remain, mainly in the Salem and Oxlandia archives. Scholars have identified the three wise men as Freud, Lacan and Jung. Each had authority over different aspects of man: his dreams, his sexuality, his ideal self. These aspects are understood to correspond to three different areas: Vienna, www.pornhub.com and *The Red Notebook*. The location of these areas is subject to much speculation. Excavations suggest the sexual paradise of www.pornhub.com was lost after the break between the real and virtual that brought about the end of the FDA. *The Red Notebook* is thought to be one of the lost books of *The Bible*. Scholars dispute whether Vienna was a real city or merely a metaphor for the dream-state of man in the pre- and FDA. See Lok Zuk Xo, *A Vienna of the Mind: Dreams and the Word of God in Ancient Earth Cultures* (Shangri-La: University of Nirvana Press) #code-ref: ÓØÖ×#1002

5   Fragments of texts by 'Milton' and 'Dante' exist in the Salem archive, including both
    the Penguin and the infamous 'Longman' versions of Milton. According to some
    meta-theologians (particularly those of the pre-lexical and quasi-ecumenical
    school) these prophetical works should be included with other scriptures from
    The Bible. 'Dante' is understood to be a collective of monks and artists related to
    and possibly including the 'twelve disciples', a faction gathered around 'Jesus of
    Nazareth'. Jesus of Nazareth was a political radical active throughout the Middle
    East at the dawn of the Judeo-Christian period and should be understood as
    distinct from the symbolic Jesus as represented in artefacts including the Da
    Vinci code and various icons from the Vatican ruins. 'Milton' is a product of the
    workshop of St Paul. Many scholars, but particularly post-Confucians, argue that
    St Paul was a key figure in constructing the Judeo-Christian mythos as a tool for
    social order and ethical/legislative power. See, for example, Baba Po, *Christians,
    Mystics and Groovers* (Patna: Bodhisattva Press) #CODE-REF: ₫Ɑꞁ₫998-89. In some
    texts purgatory is known as 'limbo' – a special dance for penitent sinners that
    required them to 'get down low' and successfully squeeze their body underneath a
    wire or pole in order to gain access to Heaven.

6   This interpretation is disputed by numerous authorities. See in particular *Pre-
    Humanist and Trans-Humanist Belief Cultures of the 1st Digital Age* (Ulan Baatuur:
    University of Outer Mongolia) eds. Phee Phi Pho Fun. #CODE-REF: ₡3yy26662

7   Remnants of this belief system endure in the various tribal communities on the
    Southern and Oriental Ice-Shelf. See Xilent Lo, *Krishna Resurrected: The Blue and
    Orange Gods of Indiahhhh* (Su-Pen: University of Saphong Press)
    #CODE-REF: XCX✪1888836465

8   The Jedi ethical code remains the most salient in Pan-American cultures, thanks
    in part to the salvation of almost intact copies of a 'holy trinity' of visual texts
    (*A New Hope*, *The Empire Strikes Back* and *The Return of the Jedi*) after a
    successful excavation from the virtual archive of the FDA. Existence of three
    other visual Jedi texts, said paradoxically to refer to an older point in time but to
    have been made more recently, is disputed, including the existence of 'Lucas', the
    mythical creator of the Jedi code. See, for example, the popularity of 'Darth Maul'
    and 'Obi One Kenobi' factions in the New China regions of the west and north
    of the American continent. See Geek-Ah Neerrdah, *Star Wars and Jedi Knights:
    The Last True Religion of the First Digital Age* (Ulan Baatuur: University of Outer
    Mongolia) #CODE-REF: ₹ÖÖⲆꓚ989-110

9   Although the central texts of Judaism and Islam were destroyed after the
    FDA, scholars have been able to identify the three Holy Cities of Islam: Mecca,
    Jerusalem and the Dubai World Mall. Judaism was structured around three
    patriarchs or Holy Fathers. Scholars of Judaism argue the patriarchs were
    reincarnated throughout both archaic and digital epochs. The last manifestations
    of these prophets were the apocalyptic 'funny men' of the FDA. They have been
    identified as Woody Allen, Larry (King) David and Mel Brooks. See Heephut Xoona,

Kosher Kings and Comic Creators: The Patriarchs of the First Digital Age (Su-Pen: University of Saphong Press) #CODE-REF: AA⚡⚲o7177-234

10   The number three is also shown to have structured mathematical and scientific world views during the FDA. Three was believed to be the first number and the first male number and a unique prime number, whereas space was erroneously represented in three dimensions. The primitive physics of the FDA, as pioneered by the cyborg 'Hawkin' and his human lovers Einstein and 'Dawkin' understood matter as having three generations, a view that prevailed for at least another thousand years following the first break between the real and virtual realms. See G Eek Lo Spod, *They Got It All Wrong: The Fake Science of the First Digital Age* (Khaiosung: Khaiosung Quantum Academy Press) #CODE-REF: ŒφDD-KK56483756

11   Also known as a 'buck,' a 'Benjamin' and a 'green-back'. The origins of these terms remain obscure. The dollar was the hegemonic world currency during the Industrial and FDA where it was used by various institutions as a fixed source of value in an otherwise unstable market.

12   A 'Ponzi scheme' was an ingenious method of manipulating the circulation of dollars to give the illusion of wealth-creation. Like most economic superstitions, it lacked empirical credibility and relied entirely on affect – in particular euphoric emotions such as confidence, optimism and a dangerous stimulant known as 'Diet Cocaine' to perpetuate itself. See T-Rotski, *How Do You Build a Street from a Wall?* (Xian: University of Xian Press) #CODE-REF: ȝⵖ𐤌ⵎⵏ𐤌9878-11

13   The Madoff Gang were a notorious clan of swindlers and pirates led by Bernard Madoff. During the FDA they effectively stole over a hundred billion trillion units of dollar value from various financial institutions and an aristocratic social group connected to visual-digital media known as 'Hollywood.' The loss of these funds helped to instigate a prolonged period of economic woe and stagnation which in turn accelerated the collapse of the FDA. Some scholars have argued that images, divorced from a stable context, began to circulate with such speed and salience that they replaced concrete items as a primary source of value and so led to the eventual over-coding and collapse of the available semiotic and technological lexis. See T-Tal Fusion, *Who Signifies the Signified? Value and Meaning in Ancient Earth Cultures* (Old Tokyo: Old Tokyo Press) #CODE-REF: ŵïvBB171

14   A 'Credit Default Swap' was a form of economic superstition. Designed to minimise risk, the swap actually had the opposite effect, multiplying risk until the perceived gap between the actual and virtual value of a commodity reached crisis point. Despite the fact that 'Credit Default Swaps' brought about numerous financial catastrophes in the build-up to the end of the FDA, most pyramid-systems were unable to change until it was too late. 'Trickle Down' was the belief that, by awarding credit-rich people greater wealth – whether virtual, symbolic or material – some of this wealth would be displaced or decanted onto those without access to such means. Although most governments in the FDA advocated this dogma, all

remaining evidence suggests the very opposite happened and the 'Trickle Down' ideology actually exacerbated divisions between rich and poor to levels impossible to imagine in our more enlightened age. We are not sure whether 'Trickle Down' was also a cult set in opposition to the 'Marxists' (see 15, below), although there is evidence of warfare and ritual sacrifice between advocates of these systems.

15 Many examples of the superstitious belief system known as 'economics' still exist. Documentary evidence indicates that the primary fortune tellers of this system – the Adam Smith Institute (a particularly atavistic strain of the belief system), Greenspan (understood better as an effect than an individual) and Friedman (also a form of torture or shock therapy) – were adopted as close advisors by various political and national groups (also typically organised according to triplicate or pyramid structures: see the concepts of executive, legislature and judiciary). There is considerable dispute as to whether 'Marx' – the most influential form of economic superstition – really existed or whether he was actually a deity created by those disillusioned with the dominance of pyramid-based economic models. Some scholars argue that in the concept of the dialectic advocated by 'Marx' and 'Marxists' as a tool for historical and economic analysis (the thesis/antithesis/synthesis) the triplicate structure is nonetheless reiterated. See Ping Pho, *The Economics Illusion* (New Kong: University of New Kong Press) #CODE-REF: ♣ʲ⏀144545

16 During the FDA, political affiliation was often determined by whether individuals were more skilled in using one hand over another. The 'right handers' were usually in the majority and as a result 'left hand' ideas were often marginalised. For a long time it was hoped that an ambidextrous individual would unify these rival camps and there is some evidence that one Blare/Blair/Blur achieved such unity for a short time. However, his followers became disillusioned following Blare/Blair/Blur's role in magnifying Christian-Islamic conflict towards the end of the FDA. See XT Xlotti, *False Prophets of the First Digital Age: Blur and the Burning Bush* (New Kong: University of New Kong Press) #CODE-REF: Hų◻ ⋧◻#110-1001.

17 See #CODE-REF: xₐℙ❶#6767

18 See Hans Handerrson, *What's The Time, Mr Wolf? The Lunar Order of Primitive Earth Cultures* (Old Tokyo: Old Tokyo Press) #CODE-REF: ÖØÓ♣#9997-54

19 The best known of these is 'Big Ben' a giant chronometer from the Industrial Age, now on display in the Museum of Antiquity. 'Big Ben' brought order to an institution called 'Parliament'. 'Parliament' acted as a safe environment for various mentally damaged and deficient individuals to act out a range of paranoid, schizophrenic and megalomaniac identities. Some scholars have argued that Blare/Blair/Blur was an escaped inmate of Parliament who, assuming himself to be a prophet or messiah, then went against his own ambidexterity by instigating a war on the largely left-handed people of the Middle Eastern region.

20 See #CODE-REF: ⊂Ⅲ77Ɔ-1056

21 A number of texts from this period exist, mainly in fragmentary form. They offer some clues as to what happened prior to the collapse of the FDA. The most puzzling of these texts is the 'Left Behind' saga – an apparent history of the last days of western civilisation, it reveals the extent to which FDA cultures lost sight of the distinction between the real and the virtual and began to interpret political events according to mythological and cosmological systems of dubious viability. See Zug Tek, *Factual Fictions and Fractious Factions in the First Digital Age* (New Soul: University of Old Korea Press) #CODE-REF: ¥ʜⱭBBoₜ980-11

SWITCHGIRLS

TANIA HERSHMAN

WE HAD ONE EACH, assigned upon reaching a certain age. I cannot be certain now, given my current age, what that age was. I am so old now, so so old, it is a wonder I recall anything at all. Those switches on the wall, they were so much to me, mother and father to me.

Where was I?

I was the youngest, of course. Only the youngest would be recording this now, the elder ones having gone off to live their lives, in ways the youngest never can.

Switch it up. Switch it down. On/Off. Off/On.

She never spoke to me. She flung her hands towards me every now and every then, signals I learned, fast, because if not the slaps came next. And when she was up, she was as if on fire, a firework, spinning and wheeling, burning, singeing. I, the smallest, the littlest, the slowest to move out of reach, stuck in my daydreaming. She was my sister. What kind of sister? A sister I was to her, a slave sister. The others ran and danced away, pinching me as they left me to fetch, carry, brush, comb.

Switch it up. Switch it down. On/Off. Off/On.

There are stories I can tell of her, the Upper Sister, how she pressed me to the wall beside our switches, held my neck in such a way that marks are still there, patterns from the wallpaper impressed into my skin. She was violence, she was unstopped, being that we had no one above us, no one to tame us.

They made her wrong, I know now, after all these years. She was the first, and the mix was flawed, oh how flawed it was! She could not speak, was that not the first sign? Should They not have done for her early on? Perhaps They were then too young too, too naïve about Their methods.

The others, less flawed, less cruel, left me with her. I was the basest rung, the step she climbed upon. Oh sister.

Switch it up. Switch it down. On/Off. Off/On.

The Middle two were pretty little things, but they still had some glitches. One had an eye that would not stay still; the other fluttering hands that men found oh so lovely until they tried to settle her, when wooing would not even make her unmove. And what was wrong with me? Perhaps only that I did not know that nothing was. I was Their success, They must have jumped up and down, They must have laughed when they made me, I know that now. Yes! They will have said to one another.

(I know not how many there were then, or how many now are left, if any at all. It has been so long since They, since any of Them, came...)

Switch it up. Switch it down. On/Off. Off/On.

And what of the switches? When I said mother's milk, did I say mother's milk, I cannot remember, but I meant it, all that we knew of mothers was from those switches. Nudge yours slightly slowly up and it would flood you, flood me, with happy. Our happy switch, when up – but limited. I imagine Them writing charts, setting boundaries, No, no, they must not be allowed happy-all-the-time. No. No. A set amount, that's all. And each switch was sacredly connected in to one of us, I had mine, the two Middle girls had theirs and she, my Upper Sister, must have had hers too. But my Upper Sister never switched, so far as I could see, because to slap and bother me, to order me about, did it for her enough. Enough. Happy-all-the-time.

Switch it up. Switch it down. On/Off. Off/On.

The last time I recall They came to see us, I was just coming off a happy. I beamed and beamed at Them as They took notes, scribbled into small machines. Upper Sister was still there, our Middle two had both found switchmen to take them home, to make homes with. Just me and her, her wildly swinging arms not aged, not slowed.

I don't know when They took her. Some time on that visit, maybe. Maybe I turned around, maybe They happied me up with some fancy tricks, but when I unhappied back I was alone.

I do sometimes re-hear some words They said: Expedience. Survive. Functionality. But there were no instructions left, notes pinned on no walls for me. Alone.

Switch it up. Switch it down. On/Off. Off/On.

There was someone once. He did a little create some happy for me. But when he moved his arms towards my face, my neck, my legs, I was flinching and twitching and seeing her, the Upper Sister, back there, and no amount of time would change that, so he walked away. And the Middle Sisters do not contact, do not message, do not come back to see how all has never changed but me older and older.

Switch it up. Switch it down. On/Off. Off/On.

Why I am all about this now, with me so ancient? It is this: Mother's milk is almost gone. I nudge and flick my own switch, and even chance the others too, but I get just a shiver, just a tiny slip of happy now and the shivers and the slips are less and less.

Do I imagine Them, still in Their rooms, still watching, cutting down my daily limits, saying, Let's see if she…?

I more imagine that I have outlived Them all, that I was not supposed to be on and on and on the way I have. They made me so well, I am so *perfect*, I am still here. But. But. When there is not a drop of happy left what will I do?

I am imagining that: the ways They might have imagined for my ending. Maybe the happys were not just that, maybe are they fuel to fuel my thoughts, my arms and legs and other parts? And now there is no more but just a drop.

Switch it up. Switch it down. On/Off. Off/On.
I flick, a tiny slip, a tiny happy.

Switch it up. Switch it down. On/Off. Off/On.
Something. Maybe, something. So so small.
Switch it up. Switch it down. On/Off. Off/On.
Switch it up. Switch it down. On/Off. Off/On.
Switch it up. Switch it down. On/Off. Off/On.
Off/On.
Off/On.

Off.

THE PLAYWRIGHT SITS NEXT TO HER SISTER

MARY RECHNER

LISA ON THE AISLE, Therese one seat in. Shoulder to shoulder. Lisa notes Therese's short skirt, red lipstick, décolletage, hair both pinned and falling. After a moment Therese removes her fur, emitting tuberose and jasmine: Fracas. Lisa's own wool sweater hand washed, air dried. The one she wears to write. Anxiety: an enduring scent.

Sisters. Shoulder to shoulder. The play not yet started.

Lisa usually waits until the house is dark before taking a seat in back. Tonight they sit in the second row. Therese folds her fur across her lap. She reads the programme, murmurs questions.

'Was the lead actress fun to work with or a bitch?' Therese often confused the role of playwright with that of director. 'Did you want to sleep with the male lead? Did you?'

Lisa doesn't answer, pretending to be lost in thought. She isn't lost. She believes this to be the primary difference between them. (If Therese isn't lost she's unconscious, or acts like it.) Other differences: Therese can make jokes, knows how to apply metallic eye pencil, and wants to be a mother. Lisa prefers loneliness to obliteration through relationship. Each interprets borders, boundaries her own way.

Lisa fears and does not climb fences, barbed wire.

Therese fears very little. Maybe drowning? Therese isn't lost, she explores. (She's slept with so many married men.)

Lisa had wanted to sleep with the male lead.

'Are you shitting your pants?' asks Therese.

Lisa squeezes her sister's forearm.

Therese responds to physical cues; she shuts up and returns to her programme.

Lisa is too freaked out to talk. She's seen this production of her play before, but never with her sister sitting next to her. Shoulder to shoulder.

Lisa fears the resentment rising from people's bodies. Some of them wish to be elsewhere: in bed sleeping, in a comfortable chair reading a book, eating something savoury or sweet, drinking wine or beer or a

Martini, seducing someone or being seduced, scrolling through emails, answering texts.

Therese isn't the only person in the theater wearing too much perfume.

Lisa understood that some people were afraid of, or didn't like, other people. They stared at magazines and iPhones while they waited for the lights to dim, even if they'd come with someone. Was it so horrible to talk to each other or to sit quietly doing nothing for fifteen minutes?

Pretend it's yoga, Lisa suggests silently, pretend you're on a mat and a young woman with a flat stomach is commanding you to breathe, to let go.

Therese opens a tin of cinnamon mints. 'Want one?'

Lisa does.

A a child, Therese sucked Red Hots, Atomic Fireballs. Therese always wanted things to hurt.

Lisa wants people to believe her play. Wants this: people's bodies in their seats, their essence, their attention, the me of them becoming, for a charmed time, characters on stage. When it happens, if it happens, Lisa feels vaguely celestial.

Shoulder to shoulder. Therese's breath so steady she could be sleeping.

People do that too, ignore Lisa's dream in favour of their own.

The house lights start to dim.

'Oh God,' says Therese, crossing and uncrossing her warm shaved legs. 'Here we go.'

THE TREE AT THE LIMIT

AAMER HUSSEIN

T HE WOMAN, BROWN HAIRED, fine lines around brown eyes in a face that's smiled a lot. Brush in hand, body in a stained painter's smock, turning away from the window. Tree shapes through the glass, branches outlined against a grey afternoon sky. Bare branches of tall trees. At the lower left corner you sense the presence of a canvas you can't see. The colours are mild, like the back of a fallen leaf.

That's the first miniature.

In the second painting, the same scene, with a slight shift to the left. You see the large canvas she's been painting. It's a seascape. Glinting water, platinum on blue; perhaps an estuary. Boats with red and white striped sails.

There's a slight smile on her face.

The third painting is of a window. You see the sea through white gauze curtains.

The first two miniatures are called *Marya, Painting*.

The third is called *Boats in Karachi*.

The exhibition takes place in an old palace by the sea. From one of the windows, you see a scene similar to one depicted in the painting.

From the exhibition catalogue:

Marya Mahmud was born in Rome in 1917. She studied art privately. She met the historian Mazhar Mahmud in 1937, probably in Paris or Berlin. They were married in a religious ceremony a year later and travelled all over India during the last years of the Raj. Marya began to paint scenes as she saw them. Professor Mahmud was an ardent nationalist and Marya, an anti-Fascist in her native country, matched his fervour in her adopted land. In 1946, a year before Independence, they moved to Lahore where under the influence of Chughtai she began to paint scenes from legends and from history. In 1947, the Mahmuds moved to Karachi where Marya entered the most prolific period of her painting.

The fourth miniature is of a woman's naked back; the canvas cuts her figure off just below her hips. She's lifting her hair off her neck with one hand; the other hand holds up a mirror. She's obviously balancing on one foot, as the other is raised, its heel grazing a buttock. You can see her profile in shadow. It's the woman from the tree paintings.

Through the window, the sea's a deep blue field, even though it's night. You can see a white waxing moon in the night sky. Stars are reflected in the waves. They look like yellow fish.

In the fifth, again a slight shift in perspective: seascape, window, woman and a canvas in view. It's a painting of the woman taking a pause from painting trees.

The two paintings are called *Missing the Sea 1* and *Missing the Sea 2*.

Between two sequences of paintings there are walls, festooned with photographs. Marya, young, before she changed her name; she was still called Maria Maddalena Serra. Marya on her wedding day with her husband, both in traditional bridal dress. Marya, in some Indian city, in a sari. Marya painting, cooking, on a bicycle, on a march, at a reception, meeting the Shah of Iran, meeting Nasser, Nehru. Marya, older, in Europe. There are photographs of the houses Marya lived in: Karachi, Rome, London, Cambridge.

From a review of the exhibition:

Marya's Oxford-educated husband, the renowned historian Mazhar Mahmud, wrote a controversial book in 1959. It was called Aspects of Myth and Legend in Islamic Society. *In it he questioned the literal existence of angels, saying the Quranic word for angels didn't denote supernatural creatures with wings but only spiritual impulses trans-mitted to man from divine sources. The iconography of angels in later Islam was inherited from the churches and from Zoroastrian sources.*

Lucifer, too: in the Holy Book he was a jinn who refused to bow to the newborn Adam, and was exiled from the Kingdom. But as he left he asked God to let him tempt mankind and give them the test of faith.

Thus in some medieval legends and poems the Devil becomes God's faithful creature, a fallen angel, banished from heaven for the sin of pride, whose mission is to sift bad men from good and select the best for God. In some of the great poet Iqbal's poems, Lucifer is both adversary and admirer. But in the Book the Devil is not the Great Enemy. He's only a whisperer and a tempter, a creature of fire, not of the light that angels are made of; a character with no power of his own and possessed of only the power that men invest in him.

'Papa left Karachi in 1961 and Mamma went with him,' their son says, in an Italian documentary made in the artist's ninetieth year. It's showing on a monitor, with earphones appended. 'Papa felt the climate wasn't right for his book and there were rumblings from the orthodox parties. In those more tolerant times it was only a frisson but he knew he'd overstepped the mark when a critic from the other side accused him of denying the power of angels. He was told he was to be transferred to a 'hardship' posting in the Gulf and he thought the time had come to work abroad. He wanted to carry out his research freely. They went together to Rome, where he worked on his book on the martyred mystic Hallaj, who some called a heretic. When an offer came to teach in Cambridge he left his government job and they set off for England. He would never have called himself an exile, but he thought he couldn't write the kind of books he wanted to, so he was in a way in self-exile. But he felt at home anywhere near a vast library, a group of intelligent students, a colleague or two to talk to – and in Cambridge he had a Fellowship and his old friend Dr Giles Hollis, with whom he was going to write a book about forgotten heretics and schismatic Sufi sects. Mamma wasn't happy away from Karachi. She painted rarely and when she started to paint again her work was so bleak.'

The sky through the window is misty. Two treetops rise above the haze, in a violet space of sky: one's tall, the other shorter. No leaves on either.

It's a winter scene. The frames of the windows are heavy, dark: painted with more detail than the mist, the haze, the treetops, the branches. The miniature is called *The Library Window: Cambridge*. There is no date.

'Reminds me of a pair of figurines I had on top of my TV in New York,' someone says. 'A God and a Goddess. He was really tall and she was little like that tree. I think they were from Bali. Then you know I came back from holiday and found one of them gone? The little one, the lady! Obviously the cleaner just dropped it and swept it away.'

Scorpions in the desert sand. Cactus trees in an empty city street. Strange-shaped skulls, bones on empty beaches. A purple-skinned woman with three heads and three star-nippled breasts. An ephebic boy dancing with a dinner-jacketed skeleton. A woman, naked, staring at a long wild cat with a humanoid face.

Charcoal sketches. Paintings blanched of colour.

These are the paintings from England that she's best known for today.

'But who has curated the exhibition?' someone asks in a shrill tone as they move from the stark surreal canvases to jauntily coloured pictures of folk figures from the fifties: 'Why isn't it chronological? Surely these are earlier pictures?'

'It's thematic and generic,' her companion says. 'Can't you see? These are Marya's watercolours.'

A deft, lightly-coloured sketch of a man kneeling, his bleeding head held in his hands. In the background, hazy figures of a throng. It's called *The Stoning of the Heretic, 1960*. You can recognise a resemblance to her husband's features in the man's, particularly his acquiline nose, but maybe that's just the eye's imaginative licence.

'Papa and Mamma had never officially separated,' her daughter says. 'He just began to grow away from her. He spent time in Iraq and time in the States with Dr Hollis. Mamma would take the ship to Karachi and spend months here. I was teaching art at a girls' school and then I married and got pregnant. My brother Murtaza was working in Canada. The old house in Clifton, with its view of the sea, was rented out and she didn't like PECHS, the suburb where I lived. Too far away from the sea! Then Papa followed Hollis to Columbia on a year's research trip and she just lingered on in the Cambridge flat, painting those desolate scenes. But then when my second child was on the way she said she wanted to move back to Karachi, for at least a year. She said that as she stood on a railway platform waiting for the London train she'd seen a falling leaf whirl by: it fell at her feet, a dead thing, all withered and crumpled – and she knew she couldn't take another cold season. Though she hated flying, she took a plane back to Karachi in a matter of days. She took calligraphy lessons and held drawing classes at home. She attended exhibitions but mostly stayed away from Karachi's other painters. Later, she taught art and French at a mixed school and later still she worked at the University. She moved back to the Clifton house and often went for long walks, collected sea shells. My brother moved back to Pakistan in 1963 and Mamma went with cultural delegations to China and Central Asia and Egypt but she never stayed away from Karachi for any length of time.'

Through the library window, you see snowflakes, whirling: but look again and they're interspersed with leaves. Or they might all be leaves. The snow on the ground is a carpet of leaves.

Look again and the leaves seem to be tossed on the waves of a turbulent sea. There's a near-absence of colour that intensifies the greyish-white of sky, the deep brown of trunks, the silver-white of flake and leaf-carpet and sea.

In the catalogue there's a detailed enlargement of a leaf.

The miniature is called *The Tree at the Limit*.

From the exhibition catalogue:

> *The miniature alludes to a legend of Sidrat ul-Muntaha, the tree in paradise that marks the limit. It is said to bear as many leaves as there are people in the world. Each leaf bears the letters of a name. In the middle of the month of Shaban, the eighth month of the year, the tree shakes and sheds the leaves on which are written the names of those who will die in the coming year.*

The exhibition opened on Marya's ninetieth birthday. She will not attend in her wheelchair but there's a message she's recorded on film.

It's November, 2007. There's a slight breeze and the sea is calm.

'The strange thing is, that Mamma made that picture before he died in 1964,' her son says in the documentary. 'He was in Iraq, with Hollis; he'd promised to come to Karachi from Iran after visiting Baghdad, Basra and a couple of places in Azerbaijan. No one knows where they were going, or why the plane crashed in Baluchistan. There were stories of sabotage and spying but there's no likely truth to any of them. The strange thing is, that Mamma made that picture as if she knew...'

The last miniature in the exhibition is also the first example of Marya's new phase: a piece of calligraphy. A leaf seen through glass, framed by a window: a retake of the leaf-detail you saw earlier, but painted in a dense gold. Look carefully and its veins are composed of Arabic letters. The catalogue tells you they spell her husband's name.

The painting is called *A Leaf.* It's on the cover of the catalogue.

LIFT UNDER INSPECTION

DO NOT TOUCH

RICHARD BEARD

I WANT TO TELL THE truth about lifts.

I grew up in a tall, narrow house. It didn't have a lift because it was built in Old Town Swindon in about 1912, but if I close my eyes and remember the squared stair-carpet, I can see about 70 steps between the basement extension and the attic extension. Four floors, three flights of stairs, no lift. Not for me.

My first time inside a lift was in my early teens, on an outing with my dad to Harrods in London. There was probably a lift in the Swindon McIlroy's department store, but as a child I only had eyes for escalators.

Stairs, escalators, lifts: ambition had me in its grip. At the age of 17 I left home and went in search of lifts.

America and the cinema and London had lifts. Old Europe had lifts, the caged elevator throwing black and white shadows as the killer approached the forbidden floor.

In more recent films, cutting to the chase, there will often be a race between the stairs and the lift. Going up, the stairs are slower, even with a one-handed vault over the corners. I have a specific film-related lift memory. It takes place in the America I covet from television, full of tall buildings, and the lift-doors slide open at penthouse level. Out into the corridor comes Kathleen Turner holding a baby. She walks towards a bodyguard protecting a doorway, throws him the baby. The bodyguard ignores the baby, which is a doll, and reaches for his gun. Kathleen and Jack Nicholson shoot him dead, but Kathleen is appalled. 'What kind of guy could ignore a baby?'

This may not be exactly how it goes, but I must have remembered it like that for a reason.

I have never been stuck in a lift with strangers, though surely that must happen. I have lived dangerously, entered lifts alone after dark and after earthquakes. I have taken lifts between power-cuts, and have not always respected lifts as places of potential danger.

This is the truth of lifts: you need to know the secret of survival.

I once lived on the second floor of a block of flats in the Jericho area of Oxford. When I brought a girl back we'd use the lift. I had a pre-prepared joke for the space between ground and second, and I used the lift because I wanted both of us to feel transported (my other vehicle was a bicycle).

Later, in the Boulevard des Philosophes in Geneva, I had a domestic lift with a mechanism that is now mostly illegal. On each floor there was a wooden door, which would open when the lift arrived. The lift itself had a latticed gate, and would only operate when the gate was manually clicked shut. It meant that on every journey the inside walls of the building were visible, undressed stone and the forgotten glyphs of construction workers.

All the lifts in Switzerland are made by Schindler. They have a captive audience to look at the maker's name. Schindler's Lift/*Schindler's List*. There may be a joke to make here, or a poignant allusion, but I don't know what it is.

In the Swiss capital city of Bern there used to be a multi-storey shop called Vaucher. This had a lift with no doors at all. The two lift compartments were constantly in motion, up one side and down the other. The customer would wait for the compartment to come along and step in, timing a delicate hop to meet the floor of the lift compartment. It was a sports store.

In Japan, I was hoping for the lifts of the future. I found lift attendants wearing white gloves, guarding the buttons and calling out the floors. There was a scandal involving a new landmark skyscraper in Roppongi. The lift doors had some kind of fault, and a boy had his head crushed and died. Or perhaps that was the revolving doors.

I could look it up, but what would that prove?

I'm hoping it was the lift, because with a lift, in the case of malfunction there is always hope. However fast the compartment is falling I can save myself by jumping at the right moment, so that I'm rising as the lift itself smashes into the foundations of the shaft. This is the secret of survival.

To be honest, when I came back to Swindon many years after I'd left, I was a little disappointed by the wider world of lifts. Up and down, a lot of don'ts. Don't talk, don't make eye contact. Don't whistle or hum. Don't eat or sneeze.

I wanted to share my lift experiences with Mum and Dad, but we were never good at talking and while I'd been away they'd adopted a little girl. She was disabled, and couldn't move except by a hoist hooked into new industrial grooves in the living-room ceiling. To get her up to the bedrooms, so that she could live as normal a life as possible, Dad had installed a lift.

It had brushed steel doors and a red-ringed button for each of the four floors of the tall narrow house I once called home. On domestic mains electricity, this was not a fast lift. Whenever anyone used it, the lights throughout the house would dim.

I told my Dad he'd never sell the house now, but he did.

ODD JOB

PREETA SAMARASAN

I T WAS THE YEAR my father got retrenched and Josephine's sister Evangline was spotted hanging around with a Malay boy at the A&W. Josephine and myself were waiting for our Form Five exam results. We thought if we had to spend one more afternoon listening to our mothers moaning about money or shame we'll go mad.

At first when we cooked up the scheme we thought we'll try the bungalows behind the market. But then swept along by our own ambition we said: Why not go for the Tenby Lane mansions? From the schoolbus every morning we used to see all the high gates and if we squinted we could catch a glimpse of some of the houses at the end of their driveways. There were about half a dozen of them all in a row.

It was hell of a bloody exciting just to earn a bit of money for the first time in our lives. Add to that the thrill of seeing inside these people's houses and we were practically high. Who started making up the stories I don't know for sure but it was probably me.

'Look look', I must've said. 'You saw or not what a handsome fler the Indian gardener is? And this Chinese *ah moi so pretty* but the husband seventy years old at least, look at his picture on top of the piano. Hmm hmm hmm.'

The old Eurasian woman in the third house even told us her name: Beryl. Small bluish eyes like diamonds. Pink silk dressing gown. A piece of raw meat was bleeding into the wooden chopping board and on our way out to water the plants we saw Beryl lift up a big shiny knife over it. I said to Josephine:

'That's Beryl's husband, you know or not? She killed him and froze him and tonight she will feed him to her guests.'

We giggled like fools even though we both knew I stole that story from all over the place. An old *Reader's Digest*, a film I saw late at night when I was supposed to be studying for my physics paper, the notorious Curry Murderess case.

The last mansion belonged to an English planter who never went back home when all the others went. If you said the English House then everybody in town knew which house you were talking about. Those who lived in that area would always mention it as a landmark. When they stopped a taxi in town they would tell the man, off Tenby Lane just past the English House, so that he could estimate the fare. You see even from far away or at night that house was easy to find: the sharp-sharp points of its big black gate were painted gold and shone in the sun or under the streetlights. From pillar to pillar an iron arch curved high over the gate and right in the middle of that arch was a stag. Like an animal from a fairytale book or a fable it was. The antlers like a tree. The front feet dancing up in the air as though it was leaping out from the forest at every moment. It was a proud and angry thing and just looking at it you thought, Wah what a grand life those people must be living.

By the time Josephine and I got to the English House we had already made up ten, fifteen stories about the planter. Running a brothel in there we said. Or kidnapping small boys and keeping them in a dungeon for his foul deeds. When the maid opened the gate itself we could barely keep a straight face.

The house was of course damn posh. Like what you see in the magazines. Velvet armchairs and all that. Even the light inside was purple from seeping through the bougainvillea that formed a thick curtain outside the windows. There was a smell that seemed to go with that purple light: something sweet like vanilla but more flowery and also cooler, not like something baking in an oven. To this day I've not smelled it again.

The maid was a skinny Indian girl with droopy eyelids and a heavy jaw like as though she was just recovering from mumps.

'Madam is resting,' she said to us. 'Madam said you can come upstairs and sort out some clothes for donation.'

She led us up into a room where all the furniture was covered with white bedsheets except for one fat cupboard. This she threw open. On the inside of one door was a dirty mirror so warped that it made the three of us look like big-headed stick-bodied aliens. Clothes – not folded but just balled up or thrown in – filled every shelf.

'All the children's clothes put in this box,' she said. All the others fold nicely and put on top of the bed.'

The children's clothes were all for a small girl and all expensive things: dresses with smocking, delicate embroidery, satin sashes. Barely worn some more.

'Just look at these', I said to Josephine. 'Practically brand new! If I took them back home for Shireen and Sheila, wah just think how their faces will look.'

'Why not?' Josephine said. 'After all they're going for donation, isn't it? That's also donation, what? Your father just lost his job.'

But I didn't take a single dress and Josephine did not press me. We were not required to fold the clothes going into the box but somehow we did so anyway. Whether it was because the dresses were so beautiful or something else, both of us must have felt it would be disrespectful to just throw them into the box. In that sweet-smelling silence we folded and smoothed, smoothed and folded. We did not say: Oh the Madam is banging the rotiman in her bedroom, or, Oh that servant girl finished off the madam and has taken her place as the planter's wife. We did not compose a single story.

Josephine was carrying an armful of clothes over to the bed when I noticed the movement behind me. I was the only one who could see the mirror at that moment and it happened so fast that I barely had a chance to catch my breath. It was the woman's thin long face I saw first. Pale but not white. She could have been Chinese or Malay or Eurasian but mostly what I noticed was the dark patch on her cheek: a green grey purple black patch, a bruise. I could have sworn I saw it but before I could catch hold of the image and give it a proper place inside my head the door closed very quietly and that crack of light was gone. Funny because before that door closed neither I nor Josephine had noticed that it was slightly ajar and yet now it was noticeably darker in the corridor behind me.

If you don't even know what you saw then how can you tell anybody about it? After our results came out Josephine went on to a private college in Kuala Lumpur and I went into Form Six at St Michael's. My new bus route did not include Tenby Lane so for months I did not see the English House. Then one day almost a year later the planter's wife's death came in the newspapers.

'Tsk tsk,' my mother said. 'So young she was! Not even forty years old. Eh didn't you and Josephine do some odd jobs in that house?'

'Yes ah?' I said. I kept my eyes on my breakfast and added: 'I also don't know, we did so many houses.'

In the newspapers the wife's pale skin was perfect, unbruised. The planter was detained for questioning and then released. The police confirmed that it was a suicide. But of course murder or suicide that made two deaths in a row in that house: the child's and the wife's. Nobody wanted to buy the place after the planter finally packed up and went back to England. For years the house sat empty, slowly crumbling, birds building nests in every opening. That high gate and that proud prancing stag began to look absurd against the ruins. Finally some Chinaman bought it and turned it into a high-class restaurant-cum-art gallery. Harrison House he called it after I suppose the original planter who built the place. Once in a while on my trips home I take my parents there for a treat. Every time I tell myself, one of these days must ask the owner if I can go and see the upstairs. I'll tell him I knew the family. I'll tell him it's just for old times' sake. There's nothing to be scared of, what? When I think about it, all the many colours of that bruise, the look in that woman's eyes, no way I could have seen all that in that blurry mirror. I must have imagined it.

NOISE

JAMES HIGGERSON

'**W**HAT DO YOU MEAN, Paul, when you say that it all got too loud for you?' Dr Sylvester asked. Paul liked her voice – it was neutral and unafraid, a tone that had been absent in recent days from those that he knew and cared for. He liked that she was a good ten years older than him; he could trust in her credentials that little bit more at a time when he was feeling uneasy about the ever-increasing number of bus drivers who were younger than him. He also liked that she was asking him what he meant, rather than just nodding like she understood implicitly. That set her apart from the rest as well.

He was suspicious of her, of course. He didn't believe that she wanted to help, just that she was professionally obliged to listen to him. At the same time he liked that. She wasn't going to interrupt, or start talking about herself instead, or change the subject onto something that weirded her out less. She'd said at the start that she wanted him to think about his answers rather than just say something to keep the conversation flowing. He liked that about her as well. Not many people could cope with the silence that a considered opinion generated.

The down side was that she was also expecting him to explain himself. He hadn't had to do that before. He knew exactly what he meant, so he'd never tried to articulate it. It just got too loud. To him, that explained everything. The loudness had been there for some time, perhaps always. It had grown in increments, until the day arrived when it was all just too noisy for him to cope. That was how he'd ended up in this deliberately comforting room, without even the rhythm of a clock to break the quiet. He'd never tried to unearth the words to define this loudness of his. But if he thought about it…

It was being jolted into wakefulness by the strains of a once-loved song turned nemesis due to its role in the five-times weekly ritual of dragging him prematurely towards the demands of a new day. It was dismissing the alarm call to be greeted by a swarm of notifications of things that had happened during the night; two missed calls, one voicemail, three text messages, five emails for the work address, two more for the personal. It was the 36 alerts of varying importance received from his clutch of social networking platforms, each demanding equal – and preferably immediate – attention, a mixture of work and personal concerns, the lines truly blurred.

It was the tinny crackle and hiss of fifty pairs of headphones glued into the ears of fifty commuters trying to reclaim personal space on public transport, mixed in with key taps on BlackBerries and the rustling of uninspired hands thumbing through the *Metro* newspaper, the readers not realising that they're being surreptitiously exposed to the *Daily Mail* in a free and digestible format. It's the sounds he put in his own ears to counteract those coming from his fellow travellers: the loud phone conversations in languages he didn't understand, the disgusting sniffles of a bunged-up phlegmbot, and that of the fucking idiot who believes that it is reasonable behaviour to be playing music out of his phone at loud volumes through substandard speakers so bad that it makes every song sound like the Velvet Underground playing at a feedback convention, whilst everyone faces the front pretending not to be put out by the true awfulness of the aural experience, knowing full well what happens to people who intervene on buses.

He wondered if that was his complete definition, even as he was thinking of further illustrations. Dr Sylvester remained entirely ambiguous. Whenever he was ready, her eyes seemed to say, if they were trying to speak at all.

It was, he continued to think, the omnipresence of news, seemingly more news than ever before in the year when the wheels fell off in all sorts of ways. The explosion of the phone-hacking scandal, which took everyone's minds off superinjunctions, itself an obsession for three weeks where the freedom of the press was supported provided a celebrity blowjob was involved, a freedom that did not extend to Voicemail burglary. Each day a new revelation superseding the last – an endless list of suddenly wronged celebrities, mild outrage, then the phone of a murdered schoolgirl, then 7/7 victims, then dead soldiers; the nation's favourite causes all abused by the press they've lapped up for years, no-one ever bothering to care who these unnamed sources were at the time, just as long as the news was salacious. The resignations from the communications officers, the police chiefs, the directors of the empire, a new head rolling with the passing of each press conference. The closure of a national institution, the supportive sentiments of a campaigning mother later to be alleged as another victim, high-profile arrests followed by higher-profile arrests, a public flogging masquerading as a parliamentary committee. The media screams louder than ever when it's talking about itself, especially at the expense of its fallen rival, a story seemingly endless in scope and duration. And this only one tale in a time overwhelmed by occurrences.

Beyond the efforts of tabloid criminals and their methods of generating news, it was the onslaught of monumental happenings at every turn. Rolling news on the television, breaking news via Twitter conjecture, bad news on the hour, every hour. It was an earthquake in Japan, an uprising in Egypt, a bloodbath in Oslo, an uprising in Libya, public sector protests, an uprising in Syria. It was the death of Bin Laden, the anniversary of 9/11 outweighing the millions of needless fatalities in the decade since, teens killing teens, the 'unsurprising but no less tragic' loss of Amy Winehouse and the public's need to validate their grief through posthumous record purchases. It was the EU-27 lining up to take it in turns at standing on the brink of financial collapse, US prosperity hanging by a thread, maximum unemployment, double dip fears, the liquidation of household names, domino-style. It was riots on the streets of a major city near you and the disproportionate punishments set to placate a livid populace, the troubles of the poor suddenly spilling out of the estates unavoidably into the conscious of those who found it easier to ignore such things. It's been blanket misery, whichever way you looked.

Not enough, he thought, gazing away from Dr Sylvester and looking out of the window to the small, tranquil garden, the opposite of the loudness he was conjuring up in his head. He had now gone beyond the reasonable thinking time for any adult and looking away from her seemed to relieve him of any pressure to say anything soon.

It was also the thoughts that he dragged with him into his morning shower, the bleary-eyed negatives that spilled out when he considered work and the knowledge that – despite anything – he wouldn't be able to achieve all he wanted to in that day, not when work would thwart his real ambitions with its soul-crushing buzzwords.

It really was work; work was the loudest of all. An open-plan nightmare of personality clashes, ever-ringing extensions and office politics. It was the ever-expanding dictionary of professional language; the brownbag seminars and blue sky thinking, the incentivisation and clear-desk policies, the transparency, the loss-leading, the motivated team-playing go-getting units of workforce. It was the suspicious way two colleagues would look at him when they were talking about him. It was having a conversation that ended, 'We must have a conversation about this,' as if that wasn't something that was happening right at that second. It was the tirade of emails he was needlessly cced into, and that cced had become a term he used in real-life speech. It was the meeting requests and training sessions, lessons in motivation and stating the bleeding obvious, deftly delivered through Powerpoint presentation. It was hearing his own name attached to sentences he wished it wasn't, hundreds and hundreds of time each day.

'Paul, can you?'

'Paul, would you be able to?'

'Paul, I need you to.'

'Paul.'

'PaUL.'

'PAUL!'

It was the standardisation of daily life, as sponsored by Tesco and Sainsbury's, and their carefully laid out convenience stores – breakfast pastries two for £1.20, lunchtime meal deal (sandwich, crisps OR fruit, and one of a selection of these six drinks) for £3, microwave meals for dinner at two for a fiver. The same choices day in, day out, varied enough to offer only the most minimal sense of personal freedom.

It was being organised entirely by an electronic calendar, the only distinction between work and play being in the colour-coding of each event, be it gig, lunch date, breakfast meeting or late-night teleconference. A lifestyle monitored and controlled by Microsoft Outlook, the software gradually taking over his primary mental functions. It was the relinquishing of personal responsibility to a handheld gadget that became more essential with the downloading of each new app, not just a luxury but an absolute necessity, more vital and central than any one person could be in his life.

Although he couldn't feel it outright, not like a few days before, Paul could sense the combined stress of these thoughts. The deeply entrenched uneasiness was there, spreading in the way he imagined cancer might, from the stomach and upwards to his chest. Despite the moisture evaporating from his mouth, and the way he nervously brushed the first and middle fingers of each hand against each other, he wasn't done, and now he'd started, he wanted to know what he meant. Paul glanced back at the doctor, who remained stoically patient, paid to wait.

It was the permanent need for instant gratification. It was the 'where r u?' text message received from a friend less than a minute after the allotted meeting time. It was finding the answer to every question on Wikipedia; the death knell for inquisition and discourse now that trivia was at everyone's finger-tips. It was the text message received to tell you of an email directing you to a wall post that required an instant response and – if possible – a retweet.

It was the combined holler of artificial noises; distal sirens, car horns, ringtones, traffic lights, alerts. It was the increasing frequency of conversations with machines, slowly outnumbering good old human interaction.

'In four hundred yards, turn left.'

'Unexpected item in bagging area.'

'Cashier number 3 please.'

'After the beep, please state your postcode.'

'I'm sorry, I didn't quite catch that.'

'The – 15.42 – train for – Blackpool North – has been delayed by approximately – 79 – minutes.'

It was the thunderous growl of thousands of people per second becoming enraged with supermarket self-service machines, answering back to a mechanised voice with a range of only ten or twelve sentences, yet never managing to win the debate.

It was the fear of silence, as if the quiet were a shortcut to loneliness. The need for background music, background television, background conversation. It was playing solitaire whilst watching television, updating Facebook whilst speaking to his mother on the phone, text messaging whilst dining with another friend, halved attention disguised as multitasking.

It was the city centre slalom, avoiding chuggers, preachers, performers and insurers trying to make eye contact despite his unfriendly expression. The bright, tenacious young things running at him with their perky breasts and warm smiles, using flirtation to try and lure him into a charitable direct debit, for which they would be rewarded with a handsome commission, playing the guilt card whilst profiting right from the mouths of the needy they were feigning concern for on that particular week. It was Clubcards, Nectar cards, Advantage cards, Costa cards, credit cards, store cards, cash cards, donor cards.

And that was it, Paul thought, for now. It just got too loud. My mind just got too busy.

He looked at Dr Sylvester just as she glanced down at her watch. Time was nearly up and it didn't seem right to end the session without an answer.

Paul smiled at Dr Sylvester. An all-knowing smile.

'Shh,' he replied, placing a finger on his lips.

A JOB WORTH DOING

SJ BUTLER

HER DAUGHTER HAD LAUGHED at her for coming. Over dinner, she'd said, 'Why bother, Mum? They've all gone. No one will know.'

But she would know and in all these years she's never missed a day, so here she is outside the town hall, bundled up against the winter rain, a cold drip off the portico inside her collar, rootling in her handbag for the key that's in her pocket.

It's odd being here alone. The foyer is silent and lit only by the streetlamps outside. Strips of rusty light climb through the windows, cross the floor, slide over the reception desk and crawl up the back wall to touch the portraits. They alight on pale noses, ears, foreheads and chins, revealing a row of men in suits, all facing front, jaws jutting, eyes stern above serious hands.

On the bus on the way here she'd looked down at her own hands: the left folded over the right, calm on her lap. She'd straightened her fingers and seen ripples spread from knuckles to wrist, a miniature beach with row upon row of tiny sand-waves left by the retreating sea. The skin on her hands gives her away. It's not the skin of a mayor or a councillor.

Her trainers squeak as she climbs to the first floor. When she started here, it was her job to clean these stairs and all the toilets. A test, she learned later, to see if she would stay the course. She's swept the hair and skin of thousands, gathered leaves blown in on autumn gales, mopped muddy footprints from the marble, scraped shit from every surface of a cubicle. And yes, she'd rather have been the one dropping almond thins on the mayor's carpet, or leaning her forehead on the window, leaving that tell-tale small semi-circle of face-grease for someone else to wipe clean. But in the event, she's been proud of what she's done.

She stands in the mayor's office looking out over the city. It's dark, but London dark, charcoal on a toxic orange canvas. Constant movement. Tail lights sweep red tracks across the wet tarmac. Three buses wait in line at the crossing, engines grundling. Below her, people dive into the corner shop out of the rain. Their legs scissor tonight's *Standard* poster, 'Town Hall closes doors.' They've no idea she's up here.

She turns from the window: it's time for work. She has her routines and she has every intention of sticking to them. She'll do just what she's always done. Dirt falls, even in an empty building.

She starts at the far end of the corridor, working back towards the mayor's office. Dust first, then polish, vacuum once the dust has settled. The bins are full – everyone's cleared their desks, so she gathers stubs of notepads, empty biros, sweet packets, fluff, old floppy disks, phone lists, rubber bands, conference name tags, birthday cards, photos. Several doors have dark rectangles where the last occupant unscrewed their name plate.

The mayor's name plate has gone too, and the wall behind his desk is a patchwork of shaded squares, each marking where a photo hung: the mayor shaking hands with Princess Diana, the mayor arm in arm with Elton John, the mayor grinning back at Tony Blair, the mayor in a sea of waving schoolchildren, the mayor with face surprised by flashbulbs and friends and enemies and fame. Sometimes she would exchange words with him if he was still in his office when she came to clean. He seemed polite enough, pleased to see her.

She dusts, polishes and vacuums, the room is nearly done. She's saved the best till last. The mayor's office has a table. It's huge, its lines elegant but not fancy, and it has been here far longer even than she has. She believes it's oak – underneath, where it has never been polished, it gleams silver. Its maker carved his initials into the wood and as she does every time, she reaches under and feels his mark:

WP
1831

She doesn't know who WP was, but hopes he knows she's cared for his table all these years.

She takes her duster and circles her way up the table, inspecting it as she goes, checking for coffee stains, pen marks, indentations. This is where the real business was carried out – never mind the council chamber with its chairs for the public and its minute-takers. In here is where decisions were made, deals were done.

She runs a hand over the table. It's aged far better than she has. She opens her tin of beeswax, bought for this table alone. Its warm summer scent rolls up. She folds a fresh cloth into a nub, twists it into the wax, and begins to polish, rubbing hard. Her fingers start to ache but it's a good ache. Like kneading dough, the movement is repetitive, circular, powerful, it frees her mind and lets her focus on the one thing. And now she takes another clean cloth, and she swings along the table, polishing, rubbing, stretching her arms across, sweeping all before her till she arrives back at the mayor's chair and stands triumphant. She loves this table.

After a moment, she crosses to the door. She passes the phone on the mayor's desk and lifts the receiver. She thinks of the wires running from it like veins through the building, and listens to its silence for a minute before she places it on its side next to the phone. She clicks off the lights.

She returns to the head of the table and sits, her hands flat in front of her, palms down, wax-sticky fingers jagging against the table's polish. They glow in the iron light from the streets outside. She shuts her eyes and pushes her fingertips over the wood, feeling its grain, its delicate solidity.

She breathes slowly, hearing the room settle around her into stillness.

There's no hurry tonight, no watchman to shoo her home – she'll stay here, keep the place company.

Her mind begins to spread into the spaces of the building, down corridors, behind curtains, into rooms she's never seen, workshops, storerooms, shelves and shelves of documents, maps, plans, decisions. She lets it wander.

Gradually, she feels small sounds.

The closing of a door.

The whisper of a file sliding back into its drawer.

The clatter and ping of typewriters.

They stroke her shoulder, blow across her fingers, tap her teeth.

A note rises from the piano two empty floors below her. She breathes out, lets it in.

Then another note and another, singing through her membranes, beginning a slow thrum in her veins, a steady pluck in her guts, till the building's whole symphony runs through her, fills her, expands her, is more than her, and as she opens her mouth and laughs, they rise, they rise out into the sky, a flock of starlings swirling up and over a rooftop.

SERE

DAVID ROSE

I HAVE JUST BEEN LOOKING at some shoes. There's a little Italian shop round the corner from the office. I'm not contemplating buying any; these will see me out. Nice though to admire the cobbler's craft in an age of canvas.

These were exquisite: the contour of the toe; the marbled leather of the vamp; the hand-stitching of the sole.

But another pair caught my eye, though not my taste. Of similar design but in two-tone leather – beige, with pearl grey vamp. What we used to call 'co-respondent shoes'. Never hear the term now. Or rarely.

I did however see reference quite recently to what they incorrectly termed 'correspondent' shoes. They clearly didn't understand the term, thinking maybe of expense-account journalists. (Is journalism still considered a louche profession? One rather hopes so.)

No, the term is *co-respondent*. They were worn for eminently sensible reasons, by men whose profession it was to escort unhappily married women on assignations in seedy hotels in order to secure for the woman a divorce on grounds of adultery.

Naturally, the more *outré* the shoes left in the corridor overnight for the Boots, the stronger the evidence in court on the part of the house detective.

All disappeared now. With Divorce Law Reform it became redundant. The time will come – may have done so already – when no one will recognise the term. For who now remembers Blakeys in an age of rubber soles?

I mention all this in justification of my melancholia. Another little jolt to one's self-esteem, reminder of the discrepancy between inner- and outer-chronological grasp.

And yet, in counterbalance, I still feel quite sprightly, despite having been on my feet since around ten am (I nearly said *ack emma*). I've been back to the office. I say *office* – in fact there are two, old and new. I alternate.

Today was the old. Deserted, to all appearances, but that's no deterrence. I can wander happily round, remark the paint chips on the skirting board (from when I qualified for an 'Executive' desk, with full side drawers), listen for hidden laughter, catch a trace, or imagine I do, of the olfactory presence of Sylvia Allthorpe – that heady concoction of Drene shampoo and 'Night In Paris'; linger for a while in the corridors of what-might-have-been had it not been for my overdeveloped sense of... tact.

But one can't, as they say, live in the past, and I feel as much at home in the new. Almost. I drift in, they don't seem to mind, tolerate my presence, even though I recognise few of the staff and none recognise me.

Some of the procedures are still familiar to me, though even Planning is now all computers. I have difficulty following the lingo.

I remember, many years ago, in my years of exploration, becoming fascinated with Nuclear Physics – Quantum Theory, Relativity, Heisenberg and Schrödinger. A purely lay interest, of course, as it had little or no application to Forward Planning, Drains & Lighting. Fascinating nonetheless.

And what was most fascinating to me was the terminology, the proliferation of new terms as the foundations of matter ramified further. *Quarks, electrons, positrons, neutrinos...* Each discovery demanded yet more neologistic ingenuity. Thus built up a lexical index of the world's increasing strangeness.

I'm reminded of that as I watch their computer screens, listen in to the banter and shop talk. One feels a duty to keep abreast, but...

I thought I had caught a glimpse of her once, stepping out through the automatic doors. I followed her. I realised quite soon my mistake – how could it have been? But no matter, this woman too had that same elegance, same refinement bred of disappointment. What if, with the confidence of maturity...? I tipped my hat; she failed to respond. Then was lost in the jostle of Russell Square, and I continued, as today, to my train, the dead metallic leaves rattling against the railings; down the escalator, to be warmed by the old familiar draught through the tunnel.

My luck has held today, too. There's a single seat in the corner of the carriage. I just manage to slip ahead through the doors as they open.

Sink into the seat, wedged safe against the window, bask in the torpid warmth...

Darling, there's one free seat in the corner. You take it, I'll stand.

MORAYO

SARAH LADIPO MANYIKA

THIS YEAR, SHE BUYS a pair of red suede shoes. They are not cheap, but they're gorgeous. They have a sensible wedge heel with a peek-a-boo toe and on the outside they are a deep, plush scarlet red. It's a big birthday this time, which is why she matches the shoes with a black chiffon dress, and her double string of pearls. She doesn't own a full-length mirror, so she climbs onto the ledge of the bath and holds firmly to the edge of the door to balance. This way she sees both the shoes and the dress in the bathroom mirror. She twists for a better side view, admiring her posture.

She's lucky, they say, that a neighbour heard her fall. She is lucky to be alive. But luck, she feels, is not the right word. Not when her spine is broken and she must lie in bed for an indeterminate time, at the Good Life Residential Home. Now she spends her days yearning for the familiarity and comfort of her old place. At night she rarely sleeps. Her neighbours down the hall have nightmares and the nurses are noisy as they bustle up and down in their loose, cotton trousers and rubber-soled shoes. She tries blocking her ears, but that doesn't help, and often when she's just about to fall asleep, that's when the pipes in her room start to creak and wheeze. She longs for someone to open a window to stop the brittle heat from drying out her eyes and nose, but she feels vulnerable lying on her back so doesn't ask for help.

Instead, she waits for daylight as it drags its reluctant feet behind the smell of burnt toast that slips in every morning through the space at the bottom of her door. She closes her eyes and inhales deeply in order to summon the smell of moi-moi and akara with ogi or even porridge. *Porridge would be nice*, she whispers, as Goldilocks comes to mind. At lunchtime and dinner it's almost always boiled potatoes and once again she wills her senses into tasting something else. She imagines fresh fettuccine with grated Parmesan and shavings of pink peppercorns, or Madam Koto's spicy chicken pepper soup, with jollof rice and fried plantains. And then come Mrs Sen's curries, pilafs, nan, roti, apple crumble and crème fraîche followed by Peter Rabbit's chamomile tea. If only she had her books.

In her study back home there are rows and rows of books stacked from floor to ceiling. The books that used to belong to her mother now live at the top and at the very top, in the tiny shelves hidden behind the glass doors, are all her old Beatrix Potters and Teddy Robinsons – still waiting, sixty years on, for children. Her cookery books and magazines sit at the bottom and everything else lives in between. She used to keep some books apart on a separate shelf, but all that changed when Ezinma from *Things Fall Apart* and Nyasha from *Nervous Conditions* hopped off the shelves, on the eve of Nigeria's golden jubilee, to complain. They told her they were tired of living on the same old row with other minor characters in sad stories. What they wanted, more than anything else, was to sit next to happier women, gutsy women and women from around the world. So she obliged and moved them all around. Later, she did away with alphabetical ordering altogether and grouped her books around characters. This was how Shakespeare's Ophelia found Tolstoy's Anna Karenina and Grossman's Ora became acquainted with Gordimer's women. And with this new arrangement came the idea for her new book. She would take her favourite minor characters – Ezinma et al – and transform them into larger-than-life women who would challenge all those grumpy old men of Barnes, Roth and Coetzee now sitting on the bottom shelves. But first, she must read through her books and find the thick pencil marks made as a young student and the thin ticks added in later years. She must stumble across her old receipts, postcards and dried flowers that once served as bookmarks and now as reminders of times past. She must hold them and feel them – some old, yellow and crinkly; others young and glossy, hardly broken in, like her, once upon a time.

To Tom Harris, the mess in which he finds the old lady's books is a reflection of her state of mind. They are strewn haphazardly across the shelves, some with spines facing inward, others facing out. Nothing is arranged alphabetically and like abandoned children's toys he discovers many tucked away in clothes drawers and cupboards. Added proof, for that unrelenting social worker, that his court appointment as legal conservator is not only needed, but also timely. There is no space in his client's new facility for all these books, but he will keep a few with which to decorate her room at the Good Life. He tries to imagine what a woman of her age and background might like. He chooses two books by Maya Angelou, as he's heard of her, as well as several books from the Civil Rights era – her era. He also adds the complete works of Shakespeare, which he finds sitting on her desk. The rest he will have to sell. He hires a student to help him and tells her, because she's attractive, that she can keep a book or two if she'd like. He informs her that his client used to be a writer. A famous writer, he adds, in the hope of enlivening what will surely be a dull afternoon for this sports science major from San Francisco State. Later, he hears the student whispering on her phone. 'She's gotta be hella famous 'cos she's got all these signed copies in different languages.' He is pleased to have made the student's job so exciting.

At the estate sale, the book buyer doesn't let on that some of the books are rare and valuable. There are signatures from Baldwin and Sartre and even Virginia Woolf. He asks if the woman came from Africa, as this would explain the presence of many of the original Heinemann African Writers Series – all signed. But Mr Harris doesn't seem to know, so the book buyer leaves it at that. He pays a token amount for the sixteen boxes and on his way home phones a friend at Sotheby's. Now all that remain with Mr Harris are some children's books, a few contemporary novels and a box full of dictionaries. Jasper, who turns up at the end of the morning is happy to be given the children's books for free which he'll sell on 24th street to the kind women who always give him a couple of dollars and listen to his stories of Vietnam. He also takes the dictionaries and is delighted to find a $20 bill tucked in the page beginning with 'legacy'. He sees this as a sign and goes through all the other pages, hoping. Of the last two remaining boxes, one eventually finds its way to a doctor's reception where pregnant women browse half-heartedly through the assortment of magazines and novels. The second box is left out on the street with a sign that says 'for free,' but cookery books are not popular, except to teenage boys who appreciate the weight of these books and use the box as a prop for skateboard tricks until the cops arrive and tell them to move on.

Morayo is thrilled when Tom brings her some books (at last!) but waits until he leaves before examining what he has brought. She is puzzled when she finds the Shakespeare plays that don't belong to her and even more puzzled at his choice of African American history books that she didn't know she owned. Perhaps it is Black History Month and this is why he has brought them. She loses track these days of the time of the year, but if she can remember she must ask him about the Shakespeare plays and tell him what books to bring next time. She'll ask him for the books on the middle two shelves, closest to her desk, as these are what she needs to help her with the next book. In preparation, she requests a bookshelf, imagining one like those she has at home, but instead they bring her something barely the size of a shoe rack. She tries to hide her disappointment, but fails as the tears come spilling out. Later, to comfort her, someone brings two teddy bears and arranges them on the empty shelf. Morayo looks at the bears and wonders how many other old women's rooms these toys have visited and how many women the bears have made sadder. She thinks of her women characters now, as fragments of the new story begin to come together. When she remembers, she must tell Tom to bring those books – those books on the two middle shelves.

To Carl

delighted to meet at
last, and at a fabulous time
of year = Stamford Bridge
very much in mind

— [signature]

Roger 2012.

WAITING

JUSTIN HILL

UNTIL I WAS TEN I shared a bedroom with my brother, at the front of the house. Then I moved into the guest room, at the back of the house, which I shared with an old chest freezer, some exposed pipes that gurgled into the adjacent bathroom, and a bricked-up fireplace. The chest freezer had a tartan rug thrown over it, to keep the cold in and a red light, on the bottom left corner. But it kept to itself. Sometimes it hummed, then it would stop and think, and hum again.

There were wood pigeons who liked to sit on top of the chimney in the morning. Their call echoed down the bricked up fireplace and woke me to another grey teenage 1980s day. And there was a wardrobe in the far corner of the room. It opened onto a small squarish room, the landing of the original house which was buried in the centre of the conversion. It had been a walk-in closet for the room my brother and I had once shared. There was a false wall between it and my wardrobe, which, when you learnt to look at it the right way, was a blocked-up doorway.

And then one day, my father said he would make that space into a secret study for me.

To get there you had to push through the clothes in my wardrobe, and then into the secret room behind. I put moth balls into the wardrobe, so it would be more like the wardrobe that led into Narnia.

'Ever walk into a room and forget why you are there?' a voice on the radio asked. 'Well, new research from the University of Notre Dame explains why this is so.'

The researcher was called Professor Gabriel Radvansky. He was American and I was marking undergraduate short stories at my desk when he started to explain.

'Entering or exiting through a doorway serves as an "event boundary" in the mind, which separates episodes of activity and files them away. Recalling the decision or activity that was made in a different room is difficult because it has been compartmentalised.

'So when you forget what you are doing here, going back to the original room can rejog your memory,' Professor Gabriel Radvansky said.

26 JULY 2008, HONG KONG Setting sun throws light from behind the stern of the evening ferry from Discovery Bay to Central. Long stretch of blue water, blue hills rising over the blue freight ships with containers with names like *Wan Hai*, *TS Lines*, COSCO.

A handful of others sharing the ferry: mostly local Chinese and Nepalese workers returning home for the night.

Come to lighthouse rock: the sudden green surprises me. Sunlight gives jungle slopes a uniform green.

The harbour shore's lined with blocks of narrow white apartments. Capital 'I's – some taller, some shorter, a collection of flats looking a little lost amongst the corporate buildings that tower over them. I, I, I, I, I, I they call out, like seagulls.

Odd and dreamy moment. Don't feel like a single 'I'. My mind is drifting. Feel more like a 'we' of Justins, scattered like waves through Hong Kong Harbour. Backwards and forwards through memory and expectation, oddly rising up here at this moment, before falling forwards into the future, only seconds away.

I don't remember that first bedroom door. But I do remember the feeling of a door shut behind me.

There were many things you could do with a door shut that you couldn't do with a door wide open, or even a door a little ajar. You could read. And it was there that I read the *Lord of the Rings* and *The Hobbit* and fell in love with stories and strange worlds, and decided to become a writer. You could dream in a closed room; listen to music as loud as you wanted. You could lie in bed and listen to the radiators gurgle into life at 6.30am, when it was still December-dark outside, and wait for the central heating to take the edge off the frost.

You could wake up and hear that Britain was at war with Argentina. You could replay after-images of the miners' strike in your mind; listen to your parents next door as they shared the bath. Mwa mwa mwa, they said, like Charlie Brown's parents. Sometimes it sounded like they were arguing; sometimes you thought they were talking about you; sometimes they did argue and you could feel guilt and fear deep in your gut, where, like stomach aches, it hurt the most.

No one would bother you. You could hang the Tolkien Calendar up on your wall, listen to the *World Tonight*, scatter *White Dwarfs* by the pillow. You could leave socks on the floor, dump your leather briefcase with all its homework on the bed, you could set your polished black shoes ready for the next day's school, put up your Elmet House photo on the wall and enjoy looking at your best friend's face there standing next to you; and you could wake to snow falling in the garden, silent and inexorable, and you could trace your name in the condensation: Justin. Aged 12. Just above the Smurf sticker that came free from the petrol station.

The study was published in the *Quarterly Journal of Experimental Psychology*.

In the first experiment subjects were in a virtual environment. They selected an object from a table and exchanged it for an object on another table. They did the same thing while simply moving across a room but not crossing through a doorway. Subjects forgot more after walking through a doorway compared to moving the same distance across a room, suggesting that the doorway was an event boundary that impeded one's ability to retrieve thoughts or decisions made in a different room.

12 OCTOBER 2004, CONNEMARA Walked out this afternoon at 5.30pm. Not Martin was bringing his cows (three cows and a calf) up the moor. Had two dogs with him: a sheep dog and the mangy one with a bad back. ('I would put it down but the young lad won't let me,' he told me once.)

I'm not sure of 'Not Martin's' name. His accent's so strong it's hard to make out. Now I've asked too many times to ask again. But the other neighbour whose cottage is a little way up the hill is definitely called Martin. So we live on a steep hillside between Martin and Not Martin.

The village is a scattering of cottages strung like lights along the road, called Cloughbrack Upper. Our cottage was the one where our landlord was born, the last of 14 children, seventy-six years ago. It's lain dormant for years and when we moved in it was full of butterflies. They were in every room – deep red admirals – some dead, some still flapping. For weeks another butterfly would appear, lost and struggling against the panes of glass in the barn front door.

The cottage's named after our landlord's mother. She died twenty years ago. We will have our first two children here. My wife will stand by the white cottage wall, the bed barn door half open, our babes in her arms, and I will take a picture of a proud and delighted new mother, smiling by a scarlet doorway, under a sign that says Lady Jane's Cottage.

That house where I had my first bedroom had subsidence. Between the old house and the extension a long black crack grew slowly wider and wider, and in the end the insurers paid up and we could move out.

I was fourteen. We moved to a Barrett's estate house a few miles away to the north side of York. All the houses were one of five designs. There were no hidden spaces. All the windows were PVC double glazed. The doors disappointed me. They were brown laminates that were hollow inside, and echoed and made poor barriers to privacy.

But I had made all the big decisions in life by then. All I was waiting for now was to shut the laminate doors of that home behind me.

For four more years I chafed. The bedroom was smaller. There was no fireplace, and the built-in wardrobe had no hidden door to a secret study. It was small and modern and practical, and I despised it.

The only consolation was that we lived in the countryside. There were no buildings to block the view of fields and trees stretching beyond the river. The windows were vast panes of glass. Through them I discovered the sky and clouds. How clear the early morning skies were. How clouds drifted during the day, blotted out the sun, and how in the afternoon it rained. And the sunsets!

I did not know how special those sunsets were, until I lost them.

There was barely an evening when a chink did not let through a brief glimpse of light, and then the setting sun lit the undersides of the grey clouds like fireplace coals, and they burnt with a fierce beauty that could stop you in your tracks and you stood and forgot what you were doing and just watched, because this moment would pass, and you did not want to have missed it.

I will remember this sunset for ever, I used to tell myself. I will fix this moment in memory, and it will shine clear through the years that follow. But there were so many of them, I stopped trying to fix them, and now when I think back I do not see the moment through my mind's eye: I am like a ghost in the room, standing silent and dumb. I am not looking at the sunset or the window, because a shape is blocking the view. That shape is my younger self with his back turned to me, silhouetted by the golden light that burns in his curly blond hair. He is watching the sunset. His shape is intimately familiar because it was my shape once. He is tall and broad, but in his teens, still unchiselled. 'Unformed' perhaps is a better word – like an almost finished clay sculpture, the last grooves still to be scraped away.

In my mind he stands there eternally. Just as I did on that ferry boat in Hong Kong harbour. At the crest of one of those many moments that somehow stand out. Like the single wave in the countless acres of sea that suddenly breaks into brief foam, while all the others remain grey.

The second experiment was in a real world setting. Subjects were required to conceal in boxes the objects taken from the table and move them either across a room, or travel the same distance and walk through a doorway.

The results replicated those in the virtual world. Walking through a doorway diminished subjects' memories.

22 OCTOBER 2004, CONNEMARA A quiet morning. Made home-made crumpets. Went out to hang up washing: a few ink caps dripping back into the soil. Looking up from the lawn could see up to the next house. Sam the Sheepdog was sitting on the next house's doorstep. Couldn't see me but he could sense me and looked around.

Walked over the moor from our side of the hill today. Came up to the top of the moor looking down across the valley to Finney. Walked up to our ruin. The one we say we will buy, but never do. The two-storey walls are intact but the roof fell in long ago, and the doorframes have been removed, which gives the place a haunted moan.

Could still see the plaster in places, now white and stained green with algae and moss. Found half a horseshoe – rusted brown – and an old milk bottle in a hole in the stonework.

Not Martin and his wife and children are standing around their car when I come home. We watch him from through the open half of the barn door. After a while he walks up to our house. He knows we are in because our chimney is smoking. We hear his Wellington boot footsteps crunch across our gravel to the front door. The upper half is open. We talk through the open doorway.

'I've locked myself out the car,' he says. 'You have a Nissan too, now. Can we try your key. Maybe it'll work.'

I don't think it will work, but we all walk to look at his locked Nissan car door.

I try the key. He tries the key.

We stare at the door.

His Nissan door does not open.

My father was a headmaster of a primary school. One day I set off the fire alarm and I was sent to the Headmaster. His office door was red, and on it was a white sign with black letters which read 'Headmaster'. I sat outside that doorway for what felt like an hour, before my father finally came out and told me off.

That night at dinner, as the family sat around, my father said, 'Guess who was sent to see me today?'

I rolled my eyes.

Eighteen years later he was dead, and I drove my mother to the converted water mill where he had killed himself. He had gassed himself in the car. The car was in the garage. The body had gone, of course, the police had taken it away when they had found him. But the tulip of brandy still sat on the coffee table, next to the chair where he had last sat and looked at the view of Maulds Meaburn.

My mum wanted to retrace his steps, and I didn't want my mum to be alone while she did so. But somehow I found myself going down to the garage alone, and standing in the dark corridor and reaching out to open the doorway into the garage where my father gassed himself. There was a sudden chill. I could feel his ghost awaiting. It terrified me. It was as if I was alone at night in my first bedroom, and heard the floorboards creak and imagined someone or something was in the house. I steeled myself, put my hand on the bar of the handle – not a knob that you twist – and opened that door wide.

In the final experiment subjects passed through several doorways leading back to the room in which they started. The result showed no improvement in memory, suggesting that the act of passing through a doorway serves as a way of filing away memories.

DECEMBER 2011, HONG KONG My daughter Isabella is asleep in the room she shares with her big sister, in our apartment on the fifteenth floor of a Hong Kong high-rise. Their names are spelt across the door in brightly coloured wooden letters their Nan sent from Scotland. Isabella, Madison.

Actually, she is not asleep, but sitting on top of her sister's bunk bed, and pretending to be the older sister – and I will leave her there until her nap time is over, and she will come out and play. This little charade continues because she cannot yet open doors.

But the time will come when they will be no barrier and she will push though the long corridor of doors labelled Excitement, Risk, Danger, Dumb Decision, Adventure, Grief, Joy.

There are doorways we want to open and those we miss, and never see the other side. There are some doors we opened that should have remained closed. And there are doorways that once we pass through disappear entirely. There is no way back into the secret garden, or study.

But Isabella doesn't know that of course, as she sits on the bunk bed and plays quietly with her sister's Barbie doll, and waits.

TEN A DAY

JAN WOOLF

'**W**EREN'T YOU LISTENIN'?'

'What.'

A *what* as flat as a fart, thought Cressida looking sideways at Jake, her current sqeeze. *What.* Not even a question. No curiosity, the cunt. 'What I was sayin' just now, lover boy.'

'Yeah but what?'

Cressida rolled her eyes, showing unhealthy yellow flecks. 'About the ten hour clock.' She yelled, her jowls wobbling like liver.

'But that one's got twelve, Cress. Normal.'

'It was the blue that reminded me, not the clock. The blue. As in the deep blue sea. The English Channel,' she said, jerking her thumb towards the window, ''art there.'

'The English Channel's a murky grey, my sweet.' Jake curled his lip, revealing teeth like tiny tombstones.

'Stop being so literal,' she snarled, her own teeth – more intact – mirroring his. They looked like dogs about to fight.

'What does that mean?'

'Never mind. The deep blue sea – the MURKY GREY – of the English Channel was what Boney wants to cross.'

'Who?'

'Napoleon.'

'Who?'

'Oh, for fuck's sake.'

And Cressida stomped off to look for more dregs. She was fed up of thick boyfriends. Napoleon who! He'd have not heard of Hitler next. Too much cultural studies in the 'ome. Not enough history. Terrible really, when you think about what's going to happen.

She could hear Jake calling plaintively across the empty bar, his words fading, 'Cress, honey, babe. I'll google Napoleon in the libry, honest.'

But Cressida's mind was ticking in time with the ten-hour clock. How thrilling! To have a revolution that changed the very time. To cut two hours from the top of the clock – its crown. *Schumff*. Like the guillotine severing the heads of the aristocracy.

And for thirteen long years too. Or were they short? Were they as long as the thirteen 24-hour-day years that they'd banned? Must have been. They invaded other countries, didn't they? They weren't going to turn up like time lords – swiftly – while the others hung in their 24 hours like bits of meat in aspic. And of course, the clash and fear and stink and screams of battle would not be speeded up for the Frenchies. 'The world still took the same time to turn dinnit?' she informed Jake, now slumped against the opposite wall.

Since 1793, she knew – she'd looked it up in the libry – the new French week took 70 hours, a calendar month 300, or thereabouts. (She often got confused about calendar months, when the hostel rent was due.) A year takes 3600, so for 46,800 of their Republican hours the French lived within ten a day. And they're doing it again. How brilliant – and it's coming here. Brilliant. She'd seen the new clock outside Debenhams. 'Jake, you bastard, I seen it.' She drew breath. 'You seen it?' But Jake was asleep, having an old- hour dream. *Ten a day*, Cressida thought, grinning, reaching for the stub of Marlboro Light she'd stuffed in her pocket from the outside ashtray. How French.

But then, she knew, each hour had 100 minutes, not sixty, so they had more minutes. Hmmm. And each minute had a hundred seconds. Hmmmm. But she'll cope. Oh yes.

'I think they're on their way,' she whispered, thinking again of the Debenhams clock and that picture of Napoleon Bonaparte in the book in the libry, looking magnificent and moody, his balls tucked neatly down the side of his tight white trousers. And those top boots! That hat. 'We'll all be Frenchified now and I'd only have ten a day to cope with.'

'You fucking weirdo,' mumbled Jake – who'd woken up – as she swayed gently to an imaginary pendulum that took two Republican French seconds, so therefore a more leisurely boring English seaside town one. 'I am in the utopian concept of revolutionary time,' she told him, slurring on revolutionary, 'where anything is possible. So make yourself useful and find some more dregs you fool. Check under the tables and in the toilets.'

Jake crabbed off, checking under the tables and in the toilets.

I'll have ten a day for ever. She prised the tiny glass disc from her watch face with her fingernail, as if it was a scab. She only ever stole proper watches with faces, not those ugly digital things that were lit-up slits. Like it was a face with the brains showing. It was the face that drew you to people, wasn't it? She'd liked Jake's face at first – shame about the brains. And she loved Napoleon's. Those eyes. That nose.

So Cressida scratched out the 11 and the 12, wondering how to spend the lost hours. Or were they gained? She was becoming confused again. They'd had quite a lot of dregs and she'd forgotten her pills. That was why she had the oomph to stand on Jake's shoulder to climb through the skylight. In some places they hid in the toilets at closing time. 'Closing time,' she muttered, feeling time closing in around her. Or was it expanding?

She looked up. She wanted to hurl herself at that terrible clock face, wrench its stupid hands back – back – back to Ten. To Revolutionary Republican French Ten – when *anything is possible*. Not like here where she could just see France, a line of white vertebrae edging the beautiful deep blue sea. Mucky Grey indeed! She wants Boney to come across and carry her off, 'cos all she gets here is the community nurse and pills.

'Look, Cress, I poured some wine and some beer together. It's lots.' Jake was back with a full half-pint of dreg.

'Thank you, Jake,' she said, ever the lady. She downed the mixture and hurled the glass at the clock face – with its terrible information about the morning. A whole day to go. 'A whole 'nother terrible 24 fucking hour day,' she shrieked. 'All that spare time.'

And she felt herself going spare again. Ten hours will be so much easier, when it comes. Not long now. Not long.

OPPORTUNITY

BARBARA MHANGAMI-RUWENDE

T HE LIGHT IS GONE. We have been plunged into a dizzying darkness, hurtled into black.

'Mxim!'

My daughter Thembi sucks her teeth in exasperation from the vicinity of the kitchen table. Our bodies have memorised our two-roomed living space and we know exactly where every piece of furniture stands in the dark, which comes suddenly and often. I hear a chair scrape the cement floor as Thembi gets up. I perceive her rising out of the chair, a tall lanky thirteen year old with breasts the size of small peaches.

'I hate this country and its ZESA problems!'

I breathe in her frustration, cold and impotent. I exhale my own listless despair. Mine is a hopelessness that has slowly but relentlessly leached its way into my core, and settled comfortably there, making a home amidst the remnants of my broken dreams, which had once been fuelled by a volcanic ambition.

Darkness. It engulfs our home and enshrouds our country. It is velvet nothingness. I hear Thembi shuffling her books. The crisp rustling of paper tickles my ears, sharp and dry. A pencil drops to the floor making an infinite musical sound, which radiates in softer and softer waves into the blackness. There are no moon or stars to give partial illumination. Just darkness, as though a cosmic light switch has been flicked off. I am standing by my two-plate stove, where I have been cooking our evening meal of s'tshwala and green vegetables. The comforting bubbling of the corn meal porridge is losing its vigour as the stove cools down. I perceive Thembi will bump her head on the corner of the table as she bends down to fumble on the ground for her pencil.

Fumbling. That is what we have done and continue to do in independent Zimbabwe – the Zimbabwe of the three thousand dollar loaves of bread and ten thousand dollar packets of sugar. We fumble, stick-like fingers in pockets, feverishly digging for money which we did not put there. We pull out bits of lint and rubbish. We forage into bras, for crumpled sweaty ten thousand dollar bills which we hope we put there for safe keeping and forgot about. Time keeps moving and years pass by. We fumble in tattered handbags, inside the torn, frayed lining praying to pull out a fifty thousand dollar bearer check that may have, possibly been trapped in there. We pull out tarnished, worthless coins. And these days, we fumble for the US dollar, the mighty currency that has replaced the Zimbabwe dollar and put goods on store shelves; goods that are out of our financial reach. The US dollar, for which there are no US coins in circulation in Zimbabwe. If we buy bread for three dollars fifty and we pay with four dollars, we get fifty cents worth of sweets or bubblegum as change. Our country does not deal in coins. We deal in millions, bearer checks, US dollars and in Dandy bubblegum and Ice Mint candies for change.

'Ouch!' Thembi hisses in pain.

She has bumped her head, my gangly teenager on the verge of womanhood and the monthly rites of passage. Burdensome womanhood: inviting unwanted attention from unsavoury men who give themselves permission to see a young sapling as a full-grown tree, ready to be mounted. Tiresome womanhood: bringing with it expectations of marriage, of fecundity and of fruit of the womb. Worrisome womanhood: ushering in responsibilities and tentative, anxious dreams for one's offspring. Militant womanhood: in a state of perpetual readiness to do battle, a lioness ready to kill for her cubs.

'Sorry Thembi, *phepha ma.*'

I send soothing energy across to calm her disquieted spirit.

'Mama!'

Her voice rends the textured darkness.

'How am I supposed to study for my exams with no light? Now I have a bump on my head the size of a guava because of this stupid darkness in this stupid country run by stupid goats!'

Her words pepper the darkness, like a machine gun firing bullets into a target.

Ah! My Thembi; the one with boiling blood and a flaming tongue. I perceive her chest heaving, and her breath quickened by her anger. Her anxiety pervades the darkness. She panics as she thinks of time slithering away through the darkness into an irretrievable yesterday. Having sprouted no seedlings today, time carries on its back all promise of a rich harvest tomorrow. Darkness distorts perspective and exaggerates her worst fears. My heart aches for Thembi. What a time to be young and ambitious, cautiously carrying her fragile dreams and knowing that despite her best efforts they may be knocked to the ground and trampled upon by circumstances she had no part in creating. I feel her walking towards the small brown cupboard, feet shuffling so that she does not stub her toes on a piece of furniture as she manoeuvers in the dark.

'These power cuts will cost me my exams!' She explodes. 'I will fail and I will go blind from studying by candlelight. I will be a blind failure. That is what I will be!'

Power cuts, power struggle, power sharing. All things power dominate and hold our country in a vice-like grip. The power cuts happen at any time, silencing radios, televisions and the soft hum of the refrigerators and fans. Fretting babies become silent as night lights are snuffed out suddenly and pedestrians clutch their purses closer to their fast beating hearts and quicken their steps towards home. It is not safe, with no street lights to illuminate their path or the faces of thieves lurking in the bushes.

The ruling party and the opposition struggle for power in a bloody tug of war that lays to waste wounded bodies and maimed spirits as it intensifies around election time. The bantam weight opposition party does not stand a chance against the heavyweight ruling party, buoyed by the army, the war veterans and the police. But the struggle continues, until the ruling heavyweights proffer a benevolent hand, promising power sharing, for the good of the nation, to consolidate the gains of the liberation struggle. That liberation struggle which ended thirty years ago and whose gains are still to be consolidated. The emaciated opposition accepts the proffered hand and quickly it is gobbled up, digested and absorbed by the heavyweights. For that is what they do to opposition. We saw this some twenty years ago when the first opposition party was done away with soon after independence. They offer their version of unity in exchange for less bloodshed. Then they swallow dissenting voices and they slaughter, like chickens for a wedding feast, those who refuse to be swallowed.

Thembi has reached the cupboard and she opens the top drawer and fumbles inside for matches and a candle. She calls out:

'Mama, don't pick up that pot of s'tshwala until I light this thing. You will get burned.'

Her voice is laced with concern.

'I am waiting, my child.' I respond.

I sense that she is calmer now. She will be all right because she is learning from the mile-long queues for commodities, from the incessant power cuts and the poverty, that acceptance is the only option for survival. She is learning that to pit oneself against the establishment will cause one to shatter into a million fragments that can never be glued together. Her father's brother had his head sliced off with a single sweep of a machete during the first massacres in Nkayi after independence, for spitting into the face of a government soldier, who ordered him to fondle his own mother. The soldiers were there by orders from above to extinguish all those who spoke isiNdebele. That is how it seemed to us, though they say the soldiers were sent to deal with treasonous louts who sought to overthrow the new government. Maybe we were all treasonous louts because the killing, rape and mutilation were indiscriminate and happened if you could not understand isiShona, the language of the majority.

Her father's sister MaMoyo is broken beyond repair and she is in Engutsheni mental hospital chained to a bed and talking to people we do not see. She attended a banned opposition rally in Nketa town hall in 2000, just before elections. She was beaten to within an inch of her life. Now she stares with hollow eyes and laughs with her imaginary friends.

Thembi's father left for South Africa filled with bitterness and rage that exploded out of him and onto me, raining punches, kicks and insults that left me with a limp. He was brought back in a black bag, his body riddled with bullet holes that looked like gigantic black mosquito bites. We buried him.

Thembi is the daughter of her father's people: proud people who are descendants of warriors. I have heard her and her friends talk about the Mthwakazi Liberation Front. They say that it is a movement to fight for the rights of the Ndebele and they say they want a separate country, the Mthwakazi Kingdom. They say they want a country in which they are not the disenfranchised minority and where they will not be 'Shonarised'. I even heard Thembi tell her friends that the MLF will make sure there are jobs for school leavers, free health care, free education and improved quality of life for all Mthwakazians. I am filled with fear when I hear them talk. They are too young to remember what the heavyweights did in Matebeleland 2000, and they were not yet born in 1982. They hear us, the elders, talking in quivering voices about the atrocities, and they call us cowardly for speaking behind our hands and for accepting oppression. But they will learn that a tree that bends with the force of the wind in a frightful storm will outlive the bad weather, while the tree that resists will break. If they can bend and bide their time, they too will survive to see tomorrow, the open door to new beginnings.

Light. Thembi and I are bathed in a warm yellow glow. She smiles across at me from the cupboard and she announces: 'You can light the kerosene stove, Mama. Let me go back to my books.'

She is humming as she sits in her chair and pushes it in, scraping the floor. She leans in closer, her face towards the pages of the open book, focused and already lost in the words staring back at her. I sigh as I tighten my wrapper around my waist. I pull out my kerosene stove from under the kitchen sink and set it on the counter. The candlelight flickers, sending a shadow dancing across the wall. I glance over at Thembi, her brown skin iridescent in the candlelight. Her short hair stands up in spikes, framing her remarkable face with its high cheekbones and generous mouth. There is a frown of concentration forming ridges on her brow. Her passion for what is in those pages is reflected by the intensity in her eyes. It is as though she has an innate knowledge that the contents of those books are her doorway out of this two roomed space and the crime-ridden township, away from grasping male hands on the streets, out of the long queues for food and fuel, away from power cuts, power struggles and power sharing, and into opportunity.

IN THE DRESSING ROOM MIRROR

CLAIRE MASSEY

I DON'T LOOK AT MY REFLECTION.

When I was seven, I went to ballet classes every Saturday morning at Miss Clegg's School of Dance. The classes were held in the upstairs room of a crumbling terraced house. The floorboards were split and pitted by the tap dancers' shoes. You had to watch out for splinters. There were two mirrors, one on the back wall and one over the boarded-up fireplace, but I always stood at the barre next to the window, so I could watch the leaves on the tree outside fluttering in the wind as we ran through our *pliés* and *tendus* and *rond de jambes*. The creaky music came from a tape player that sat on top of a piano, the lid of which was always locked.

I was scared of Miss Clegg. She slapped my legs to get better turn out and said I should stop eating crisps or I would never be a dancer. She pointed at the faded newspaper clippings framed on the wall as she said that. They showed her star pupils, who had got into proper dance schools many years before. Miss Clegg couldn't dance any more. She hobbled about the room. Her toes curled upwards in her dancing shoes.

When class finished, I used to dawdle at taking my shoes off because I liked watching the older girls who came in after us, especially Kirsty Turnbull. She wore royal blue leg warmers and satin shoes. She had the lead role in the annual concert. She looked like an impossible swan. When she did her *entrechat-quatre* I really thought she might stay up in the air – her feet beating against one another – and not come down again.

The concert was held at the theatre next to the Netto car park in town. I'd never been inside before, though when we walked past on our way to the library I always looked up at the bright posters on the board outside.

Mum had to come with me into the dressing room. She'd bought me new shoes. Satin. And I had a white leotard, and a tutu she'd made from netting off the market. The older girls were taking up all the space in front of the mirrors. They lined up pots of gel and cans of hairspray on the dressing tables. They scraped their hair back so tightly into buns that they couldn't smile. Kirsty Turnbull was leaning right into the mirror to draw round her eyes with a black kohl pencil. The mums took all the chairs and nattered loudly whilst jabbing hairgrips into our heads. The air crackled with hairspray and body spray. Sitting cross-legged on the wiry carpet, I tried to go over and over the steps in my head but there was too much noise. I tried to imagine what it would be like to be on a stage. I tried to believe I could be a swan.

'The audience are in their seats. Places, girls.' Miss Clegg was wearing an elaborate green dress and fur cape, which made her look even more hunched up than normal. Her thick red lipstick had smudged onto her false teeth.

We lined up in front of the mirrors, with the littlest girls at the front and the oldest at the back. I was somewhere in the middle. We all had to dance in the opening number. When I glanced at our reflections I thought how funny we looked; pulling leotards from up bottoms, fiddling with straps and trying not to let our hands rest on the scratchy netting of our tutus. The mums all squashed past us to take their seats in the auditorium and we filed out to wait in the dark, giggly hush of the wings.

The music started then stopped. We had a real piano player for the concert. There was some muttering from the audience and then the plinking started again. The piano was going much faster than the tape player did. I tried to pull my neck up long and hold my tummy in, ready to fly onto the stage with fingers soft as feathers. The others had already set off and I had to hurry on behind them. My eyes were full of the shine of the lights. I forgot to turn and everyone else whirled around me. The edge of the stage ran down into darkness. A big black hole full of whispering and shuffling and coughing. My nan and granddad were in that blackness watching me, as well as my mum. I stood still as everyone else fluttered about. When I tried to flutter too, I found I'd missed my place in the line. I ran for the wings, where I shoved through the tutus of the older girls who were still waiting to go on.

The dressing room was empty. It seemed strange without all the noise and clutter of fidgety bodies. I waited for Mum to come and tell me off because she'd bought me new shoes and spent ages making my tutu. But she didn't appear.

I walked over to Kirsty Turnbull's mirror. There were circles in the spilled powder on the dressing table where she'd picked up her pots and cans and put them back down again. I made more circles with my finger and then examined the pale dust on its tip. I pulled it down my cheek. I didn't look any different. The mirror was covered in fingerprints and greasy smears. I leaned in closer, just like Kirsty had. I tried to imagine I could be a swan like her. Long and lean. Elegant. Not with a stubby neck, floppy wrists and fingers like twigs. Kirsty probably didn't eat crisps. She remembered the steps. She would be a real dancer. I wished and wished that it was her reflection looking out of the mirror at me. I stared harder and harder, until my eyes hurt and began to stream. I wouldn't let myself blink. My face started to fade. It went grey in places. My eyes were still there – wide and full of fluorescent light and tears, but the rest of my face was falling apart. Fragments of it spread out, away from my eyes, even though I was completely still. I panicked and pressed my fingers to the mirror, as though I could catch the pieces and pull them back together, but the mirror was solid and cold and I couldn't reach them. The chattering and banging of everyone rushing back into the room broke me away. I turned to see all the other girls smiling and jumping about. I could hear the muffled clapping of the audience. Kirsty Turnbull came towards me. I looked up at her perfect reflection in the mirror. My stomach lurched as I looked down to see if I'd lost mine completely. But it was there. All of it was there, apart from a dull patch, no bigger than a jigsaw piece, just below my left eye. I prodded the spot and it didn't feel any different, but in the mirror my fingertip disappeared into the greyish gap.

When I was a teenager, the theatre was closed and it was empty for a couple of years before they started converting it into flats. Walking home from school one night, I saw the workmen pulling loads of junk from inside. There were mangled costume rails, wooden chairs, bits of tables, and against the stone wall they'd lined up all the dressing room mirrors. It seemed strange that they'd left them intact. I pushed my face between the railings and wondered if I should go in through the gate and try to find which mirror it had been. But there were too many workmen about and they were starting to stare at me. And trying to find it would have meant looking into the mirrors, which I never did.

Even now, I avoid my reflection. I'm adept at applying makeup without a mirror and I scrape my hair back into a ponytail. I find unexpected mirrors difficult to deal with, though. Like the windows at work when I look up to find the sky has darkened with rain and the lights have transformed the trees outside into the interior of our office. But trains are the worst. I rush to get an aisle seat. I read hard and try not to look up. It's disconcerting enough to see the layering of reflections in the window – one side of the carriage over the other, the countryside from both sides running through your face, but I get pulled back to the gap below my left eye. In its emptiness it's horribly solid. In the train window nothing passes though it.

THE OWL AT THE GATE

NICHOLAS HOGG

A FTER MY MOTHER DIED Father built a wall around the house and hung a wrought-iron gate across the entrance. At the very top of the gate sits an owl. Only when the man from the village delivers vegetables is the gate opened, and only then do the hinges squeal and shriek.

Because Father is away for the war my eldest cousin, Maria, is in charge. She arrived the day we threw flowers on my mother's coffin and has stayed in the house ever since. She wears faded dresses too small for her body and my mother's apron looks like a bib on her swollen chest. Her arms are bigger than some men's, and when we go to the post office and she puts on proper shoes she's taller than my father.

Once a month my aunt visits and inspects the house for dust and dirt. She checks behind my ears for dirt too. Although it's Maria who's in trouble if they aren't clean. When my aunt has gone Maria hits me for anything she's been scolded for.

Then we go back inside and I play upstairs while she cooks or cleans or listens to the radio. We spend most of the time in the kitchen, even though it's a very big house. Everyone has left. Mother and the maid. George, the man who drove Father's car or answered the phone. Even the gardener.

I like playing games with Maria. We sometimes play whist or draughts. I beat her easily because she doesn't concentrate. I can tell she thinks of faraway places. She stares at the kitchen table, which I never used to eat at when my mother was here.

But now Maria is my mother.

We only leave the house when there's a parcel to collect, so mostly I go into the garden and watch for planes with my father's binoculars. I've seen Stirlings, Lancasters and Spitfires. The one time I climbed the gate and walked down to the brook Maria came looking for me with the man who delivers the vegetables. When they found me hunting frogs near the bridge it was dusk. She sent me to bed without any supper and slapped me so hard my cheek burned till I fell asleep.

Next morning she marched me out to the gate. 'Even if you climb over, the owl will swoop down and pluck you up like a field mouse.'

I knew it was only metal and told her I wasn't silly. She grabbed my collar and shook me.

'Remember the owl that lived in the cow shed?'

'It's gone,' I told her.

'It flew away when your mother died.'

Maria is older than me, but her spelling and handwriting are like a stupid little girl's, and she believes in fairies and goblins.

'And your father never asked them to put no owl on the gate.'

I looked at the owl, the sharp beak and pointy ears.

'God knows what happened to your mother, but if you go wandering out of here again, Heaven help us.'

One day my mother was here, then she wasn't. A policeman came round and asked Father questions. Then two policemen came round in a car and asked Father some more questions and took him to the station to make an interview.

Then we buried my mother and Father went to war.

The garden has a dried-up fountain, which is perfect for rolling marbles in the smooth stone bowl. When I get bored of marbles I go into the orchard and climb into the top branches with the binoculars and look for planes. If there are no planes I watch the fields for farmers or people walking paths to the village. I like watching them. They think they're alone, but they're not because I can see them. And this makes me feel less alone. Sometimes I see a man who looks like a shadow between the bright corn. He wears a thick black coat, even on a hot day. I've seen him carrying dead rabbits and birds.

The man who delivers vegetables wears a brown coat. He has big fat hands with bright red knuckles. He says things like, 'Bet this pile is worth a few bob.' Then he looks at the high eaves and lead windows as if he were thinking of buying the house.

When I asked why wasn't he in the war, he snapped as if he was going to hit me.

'It's not because I don't want to be. I'd be shooting Jerry every day if it weren't for me leg.'

His leg is twisted at the knee. When he walks from the van to the kitchen his whole body swings from side to side like a pendulum.

During deliveries Maria tells me to play in my bedroom and not to come out until the van is gone.

Last time the man came round it took three hours to unload and for Maria to pay him. I could hear them bringing food into the kitchen. Every time they put a bag of carrots or a sack of potatoes onto the table I heard it move across the stone floor. Sometimes the bag was so heavy the grocery man grunted like a pig.

He delivers more often now. This morning he arrived and Maria wasn't ready so he sat on the bonnet smoking a cigarette while she was in the bathroom. He flicked the butt into the flowerbed and reached through the van window and beeped the horn.

I was running downstairs to ask if he needed any help with the heavy bags when Maria saw me on the landing and told me to go back into my room.

'I can help.'

'Get.'

She shoved me through the door. She smelled of sweat and my mother's perfume. 'If I see you downstairs your backside will be so sore you won't sit down till next week.'

Then she slammed the door.

When I looked out of my window the delivery man got up off the bonnet and went inside. Even though they weren't bringing in food I heard the kitchen table bumping across the stone floor.

I played with my Meccano set until I was so bored that I opened my window and climbed down onto the water tank.

When I peeked through the keyhole Maria was riding the delivery man like a horse. His big fat hands on her bare chest.

I ran across the garden and climbed over the gate and ran down the lane to the brook. I sat throwing stones at fish then took off my shoes and hung them around my neck and walked upstream. I saw dragonflies and pond skaters. I walked until the bank grew thick with bushes and I had to pull myself up tree roots to climb out. From here I couldn't see my house. Or any other houses. Just the top of the broken windmill. I followed the edge of a bright yellow rape field until I saw a small shed and a pony kept behind barbed wire on a patch of mud. The pony came over and I felt sorry for him. His long fringe was dirty and fell over his eyes. I pulled up handfuls of grass and fed him and spoke about my mother, how she used to read to me in bed and let me sleep with her if I had a bad dream. I told the pony that my mother was dead and that Maria hated me and how she was so strong she could wrestle the delivery man to the kitchen table.

There was a small gate tied with string so I walked around and went into the paddock. The pony came over and I petted him for a while and then he just turned and trotted back to his shed. I thought that I should go back too. When I went to leave there was a man at the gate. Watching.

'I was just petting him.'

'You gave him grass.'

The man stood in front of the setting sun, a black silhouette.

'He'll have a bad stomach now. Be shitting everywhere.'

I could see yellow and broken teeth, his dirty beard.

'I have to go home.'

'Home.'

The man was looking into the distance, as if he could see someone. But there was no one.

'The Station House.'

'I know where you live.'

I wished I'd stayed in the garden, behind the wall.

'I want to go.'

'My pony'll be sick.'

'My father will be angry if you don't let me go.'

The man spat. 'I know more about your father than you do.'

I jumped onto the fence and climbed over the rail. By the time I got down the man had my hair.

I screamed.

'You great baby.'

He dragged me across the field, through a gap in the hedgerow towards the windmill. Before we got to the ruin he stopped and held me down.

'Best stop your crying, boy.'

He smelled of wee and manure.

'Been mollycoddled, ain't you? You're all soft and squidgy. Like a lamb.'

Then he picked me up, gripped the back of my neck and pushed me inside. The floors had fallen in, and the old steps were just beam ends jutting from the wall.

'Little Lamby Boy,' he said, pinching my cheek. 'I'll learn you.'

I told him to let me go, that my father would get him. But he just laughed, grabbed my shoulders and turned me around. 'See there.' He pointed up to the rafters. 'There's a nest I can't reach. You get up that beam and bring me them eggs.'

Right at the top of the tower, wedged between the beam and the roof, was a bundle of twigs.

'Go on.'

He pushed me in the back. I wanted to climb just to get away from him, and started up the rotten staircase. When I stopped and looked down he said, 'Move it, Lamby Boy.'

The stairs stopped before the nest, so I had to climb onto the beam and crawl across. It was covered in droppings and splinters, as if someone had hacked away at it with a knife.

'How many?'

Although it was nearly dark, the white eggs glowed.

'Three.'

I picked one up, and then dropped it. It cracked and splattered on the floor.

'Idiot. Put em in your pocket.'

If I fell, I'd crack and splat like that egg. My hands wouldn't move. I couldn't let go of the beam.

'Hurry up.'

I wanted my father, my mother. I cried again and the man shouted at me. Then he went very quiet.

An owl had fluttered in through the open window and perched on the opposite rafter. Bright yellow eyes and triangular ears, the razor-sharp beak. It seemed to look at what was happening, before shrieking and swooping on the man. He flung up his arms and swore, fought the owl from his face. I crawled along the beam and climbed down the staircase, running past the talons and his flapping hands, ducking the great, beating wings.

I ran across the dark field, away from the shriek of the owl and the crying man. Terrified that when I got home to the gate, the owl would be gone.

STILL

SL GREY

I REMEMBER COMING HERE with Rae and Mom and Dad. Rae wore the Wellingtons with the kitten faces that she'd got for her fourth birthday. It was still cold and wet; the first open weekend of the spring. Mom made me wear a scarf because I had the flu.

Rae and I had been so excited to come to the funfair we could hardly sleep. We left home early and when we got here the rides were all closed. The men who worked here sat smoking, drinking coffee, looking at us, but not starting the rides. Dusty tarps over all the rockets and ducks.

'What time do you?' Dad said.

One man shrugged. 'Eleven?'

Dad swore under his breath.

'Let's get some coffee. Ice cream,' said Mom. 'Surely.'

The beachfront promenade was as quiet as the funfair, the colours looked more like that time in hospital than the lights and bright of last night's dreams. Scuffed, dirty.

But right at the end, we found a kiosk with a handpainted board outside.

'RAFFLE' in big red letters, a flaking yellow star.

'Do you. Have you got?' asked Dad. I didn't see who he was talking to, but we sat on the edge of the boardwalk looking at the flat grey sea and then they had coffee and Rae and I had milkshakes.

Gull flew by, but I didn't know him then. The day got better. The doors opened and the music came on and the men stopped smoking and started pretending to smile. More children came, more families and Rae and I felt happy.

I remember the little train. Rae wanted to go again and again, but I found it boring after two goes but Mom said, 'Look after your little sister.' I sometimes wish I hadn't fought with her, because I miss her. But I wanted to go on the Ferris wheel, and the bumper cars, and Rae was too small. I wanted to go on the Hydra, most of all.

We had chipsticks for lunch, and candy floss. Dad said, 'Do you really think?' and Mom said, 'Come on.'

I went on the Hydra after lunch, when Rae was tired and happy to stand with Mom at the fence. One time. Two times. Two times should have been enough. I knew, even during that second go that I wouldn't enjoy it again. It went up too fast, and bumped down so that my bum hurt. But all the other kids were laughing and screaming, and Mom and Dad and Rae stood and smiled and waved. All of them smiling at the same time, looking at me.

I remember their faces, even though they've been gone for so long. I had some friends, in between. Rat used to come when there was still food to collect. Now he doesn't any more.

Gull says they'll open again when it's warm, that people will come back. Maybe Mom and Dad and Rae. But it's been summer and winter and summer again, and nobody has come back. Everything's closed, even the kiosk where we got those milkshakes. That painted board flakes by the ill shutters. I imagine sitting there sometimes, looking out to the flat, grey sea. I imagine sitting with them, but it's not the same.

I remember how the Hydra fell, how the sound of the children's screams changed all at once. Just enough to know, this time we weren't coming back up.

I sometimes imagine I'm riding that train with Rae forever, holding her in my lap, the smell of her hair in my nose.

Gull says they'll come back, but I think they're gone, and I'm still here.

HOW TO MAKE A ZOMBIE

DEBORAH KLAASSEN

UNI WAS A BIT of a disappointment for Tatty. She'd expected to meet intellectual challenges and friends for life, but during the first term, she found that her professors were blasé and her classmates were more interested in getting wankered than getting As. Everything about the lectures seemed to discourage debate – from the simplicity of the subject matter to the hangovers of the few fellow freshers who bothered to show up. It wasn't long before Tatty lost the urge to do well on her tests, attend lectures or indeed get out of bed before noon.

The first year raced by leaving Tatty with the suspicion that she would have learned a great deal more if she had spent the year working as a refuse collector. She was seriously considering this change of career when she met Perkins.

It happened during exam time, after the library had been evacuated because of a fire alarm. Tatty had been hiding in the library loo on the fifth floor, and when she came out, she was surprised to see the silhouette of a trench coat at the far window.

'This place feels so much more sacred when everyone is gone,' the trench coat said.

As she came closer, Tatty recognised one of the philosophy lecturers. Daniel Perkins was a minor celebrity on campus for having two PhDs at the age of 26, and for refusing to teach first-year students because 'their stupidity might be contagious'.

'Not everyone is gone,' said Tatty.

'Aren't you afraid of the fire?'

'It's only a drill.'

'You have a problem with authority.'

'It's just such a waste of time,' she said. 'Why are you still here?'

He turned away from the window. 'It's only a drill.'

Searching for something to say, Tatty watched students crawl over campus like lice on a child's skull. Fire marshals in yellow vests were trying to stop small but steady streams of students from leaking into the Students' Union. Tatty shook her head and said: 'Just look at them.'

'That's meant to be Britain's future intelligentsia,' Perkins agreed, 'yet all they do is sleep, drink and procrastinate.'

'I know. Don't they have any dreams?'

A clock chiselled the excess seconds away. Half a minute went by. Maybe more. Tatty lost count.

'In Haiti, sorcerers use spells and magic potions to turn people into zombies,' Perkins finally said. 'In the Western world, we've got clocks.'

'Are you a sorcerer?'

'Do I look like I am?'

She chuckled. He joined in. Together they laughed until, way below them, the fire drill came to an end and the lice started making their way back to their books and computers.

They exchanged jibes and phone numbers over cappuccino at the campus café that afternoon, but it wasn't until after exam time that they met up again.

Perkins showed her to the loft of a derelict school on the edge of campus. He said that was where he lived. The corridors were lined with countless coat racks and their footsteps echoed in the staircase. From hooks in the ceiling, odd objects were hung down: exercise rings, empty light fixtures and a stopped clock with a bunch of electric cables wrapped around it. Perkins had built book cases out of cardboard boxes. Tatty scanned the spines but saw titles only in German, Greek and languages that she couldn't identify. Perkins put two steaming bowls of tea on the floor, sat down on a cardboard carpet and crossed his legs.

Tatty seated herself on a stuffed sleeping bag and smiled. 'I really like your place.'

'Two years from now, the university will buy the land off the council, knock down the building and replace it with hideous student accommodation.' It struck Tatty that there was no melancholy in his voice.

'My exams went very well,' she said eventually. 'Thank you.'

'You wouldn't be here if they hadn't.' He was wearing a black turtleneck jumper and designer jeans.

'Have you been checking up on me?' she asked.

'Of course I have,' he said. 'I like what you did for Metaphysics – a transcendent fairy tale rather than an essay – but you will fail. Alisdair won't be able to appreciate your sense of irony.'

'Transcendence is bollocks,' said Tatty. 'If you can cross a border, the border wasn't really there in the first place. And if you cannot transcend it, how do you know there even is another side?'

'Like I said: you have potential.'

'Whatever that may be. So what have you been up to, lately?'

'Working on my Parmenides translation, mostly. My book on his fragments is due in December.'

'How do you do it?' she asked.

'Oh, I'd love to go into detail. Can you read Ancient Greek?'

'No, I mean, how do you do it? You seem to make so much more of your time than most people.'

He pressed the palms of his hands together. 'Sorry, what's the question exactly?'

'You know: where do you get the time?'

'What makes you think time is something you can get somewhere?'

'Well, you seem to have a lot more of it than most of us.'

'In what way?' he asked. 'Do I have more time than you, the same way you have more tea than I do?'

She picked up her bowl, noticed that it was growing cold and finished it. 'No, of course we don't own minutes, hours or days. We share them, they surround all of us'.

'Do they?'

'How else would you put it?'

'You've fallen into the metaphysical trap of seeing time as an objective, linear dimension,' he said. 'But that idea is a curse that distorts who we are and everything we do.'

'Oh really?' Tatty asked. 'And you managed to break the spell?'

'As a matter of fact, yes, I have. It's very simple; I'm surprised nobody else thought of it.'

She was quiet for a while, contemplating which question to ask first. 'Have you told anyone?'

'Nobody asked.'

'Will you tell me?'

'If you want, I can show you.' He rose from his cross-legged position without using his hands. 'You know this exercise for your upper legs, where you sit on an imaginary chair while pressing your back against the wall?'

'I think so.'

Perkins started fumbling with the clock. 'I want you to do it while timing yourself.'

'Is that clock even running?'

'I'm changing the batteries right now.' When he turned back to her, it was ticking loudly. 'When you're ready.'

With her back against the concrete wall, Tatty could feel Perkins' eyes on her body, making her legs tremble at 29 seconds and forcing sweat out of her pores at 36. At 43, she gave up.

'Not bad,' Perkins said.

Tatty rubbed the muscles in her legs. 'Now what?'

'Now we have another cuppa.'

Sat on the sleeping bag sofa, they tore ethics off its philosophical pedestal together, until the clock caught Tatty's eye again.

'Gosh, is it that late already?' She rubbed her hands. 'I should be heading off soon.'

'Not before you give it another go,' Perkins said.

'Sorry?'

'The invisible chair.' He got up and tapped the side of the clock, making it sway on its chord. 'See if you can break your own record.'

'Oh, right.' she said, 'of course.'

Tatty waited for the second hand to reach 12 before she took her place against the wall again.

'Last time, you did it for 43 seconds,' Perkins said.

Tatty kept her eyes trained on the clock. Fatigue started to eat at her muscles at 17 seconds, and at 24, she noticed that she had been holding her breath. As she exhaled, her legs almost buckled. She steadied herself with the palms of her hands against the wall until sweat started trickle from her armpits. She closed her eyes and bit her lips. I'll hold my breath again, Tatty thought, I'm too close to give up now. The hand slid past the 8. I know I can do it, I've done it before. She breathed in just that little bit deeper, swallowed and let her back slide down the wall.

'Forty-three seconds again,' she panted, 'sorry to disappoint you.'

Perkins squatted down next to her and put his hand on her knee.

'That's what you think,' he said, 'and that's why you can't do it. You just need to believe in yourself.'

'Bollocks,' she said. 'I can't do it.'

'But you just did!'

'What are you on about?'

'That clock,' he smiled, 'is rigged. The second time, it was ticking more slowly. In "normal" time, you just did the chair for 64 seconds, love.' He waved his mobile phone in her face to show that he'd been keeping track of real time.

Perkins talked for a good while longer about relativity and how he'd taught himself to mistrust clocks and rely on his own, inner rhythm. His words slowly but surely rubbed away her cynicism, and when he offered her personal training, she simply asked when he would be expecting her.

'When you're ready,' he said. 'That's lesson number one.'

♣

The next morning, the crisp smell of spring crept in through Tatty's open window, waking her up much earlier than usual. She sang in the shower ('I Want to Break Free', by Queen) and put on a second-hand summer dress that she'd recently bought on eBay. As she smoothed the creases with her palms, the fragrance of someone else's washing powder made her smile. It was the smell of a fresh start. Perhaps Perkins would make her expectations of uni come true after all.

The front door of the old boarding school was open. Tatty tip-toed up the stairs, trying not wake up the echo. In the loft, Perkins stood with his back to the door, on one foot. The right foot was placed against the inside of his left leg, just above the knee.

'I like the dress,' he said.

It took Tatty a moment to realise that he'd probably seen her through the window as she approached the building. 'Thanks. I didn't know you were into yoga.'

'Feel free to join me.'

Tatty glanced at the clock. It read nine-thirty, which was about right. Perkins lowered his arms, turned to face her and pointed at a blue yoga mat and belt that were positioned directly underneath the exercise rings.

He instructed her to lie on her back, close her eyes, flex all her muscles, relax them again and listen to the ticking of the clock. Tatty did as she was told and Perkins started to speak.

'This,' he said, 'is a lie. Clocks don't have to determine the rhythm of your life. I will teach you to mistrust clocks and rely on your own rhythm. You already know that some "minutes", "hours" and "days" take longer than others, but right now, the rhythm of your life is distorted and out of control. Eventually, you will learn to slow down seconds, minutes and hours that are valuable to you. But for now, the opposite – fast-forwarding boring or unpleasant moments – is much easier. People do it all the time. But being aware of how you do it is the key to gaining control over your own life. Are you ready?'

Tatty nodded.

'Okay. You can open your eyes now and stand up.'

Perkins guided Tatty through a series of stretches and poses with the exercise belt before he lowered the rings to shoulder height and asked her to pull herself up.

'Now put your legs through the rings,' he said, 'and let me push you, as if you're on a swing.'

Tatty tucked her dress between her legs as she followed Perkins' instructions. When she was in the desired position, he placed his hands on her lower back and pushed her gently. She closed her eyes and listened to the clock as she swung back and forth.

'Breathe as naturally as possibly,' Perkins said, 'but pay attention to what's happening.'

The swinging motion made her relax. Her lungs filled with air as she swung forward and halted at the tipping point, then deflated when she was on her way back. The clock had lost its control over her breathing.

Mid-air, something knocked her off balance. She had been expecting Perkins' hands in her lower back, catching her before pushing her forward again. Instead, they came from the front, whacking her hard. The ropes slipped out of her hands and she slammed backwards. Her spine clicked several times.

Hanging from the rings by her knees, with her head just a couple of inches above the floor, she heard herself shriek.

'What the fuck?'

From behind her, Perkins forced her feet towards her bottom and tied each ankle to the leg with the yoga belt.

'Let me go!' Tatty wriggled and arched her back, trying to work herself into a handstand or grab his feet, but Perkins caught her hands and used the loose end of the belt to tie her wrists together as well.

She screamed, but the building was abandoned and, as exam time was over, so was the nearby campus.

Perkins stepped aside, took off his sweatpants. Wide-eyed and hanging upside down, all she could see was that he wasn't wearing any underwear.

'What I am about to do to you,' he said, 'is going to be very unpleasant. Your instinct will be to slow time down, in the hope that you will find a way to make it stop. But you really don't have to stretch time, because there is no escape. The only thing you can do to make it stop is fast-forward the experience.'

'Please don't do this.' Tatty could barely hear her own voice. 'Please don't.'

'Life is like television,' he said. 'If you don't want this to happen, skip it.'

Tears ran over Tatty's forehead as Perkins pushed her knees apart and ripped the white knickers that she was wearing underneath her new summer dress. She tried not to believe what was happening. She tried really hard.

'I'm teaching you something,' Perkins panted, 'you asked me to do this.'

But no matter how hard he pushed and thrust, he could not break the metaphysical jaws of time that were crushing Tatty's hopes and dreams. Petrified, she did not learn to fast-forward time. Instead, Perkins drove the teeth of the experience deeper and deeper into her flesh, trapping her in the moment for ever.

For Hoagy Carmichael

WINTER MOON

XU XI

YOU PLAY HOAGY'S MUSIC, listen to multiple renditions of the songs he wrote. You think you know something because you've played 'The Nearness of You' so many times that it flows from your fingertips, improvises, transforms, flies.

It's winter on the South Island which means it's summer in New York and New Jersey, where the man in your life spends his nights and days. You do this distance thing because you've bought a 'crib' in New Zealand – even though you're not Kiwi – and the first piece of furniture you install is this very heavy, used upright. Its left front wheel has since fallen off, and the piano has been in a 'lock up' – more quaint Kiwi English for the room sealed off from the rest of this getaway house-crib – to rent out in your absence for over two years now. But that's another story in the yet to come, as the future articulates in Chinese.

So it's winter on the South Island and you're playing the piano in the green room. You had it painted pale green to match the garden. The painter should have been an artist, as should the gentleman contractor who restored your little villa (more quaint Kwinglish) to its former glory. You say bungalow, I say villa. *Let's call the whole thing off.*

It had been some years since you owned a piano. Having moved your life from Hong Kong to New York to be with the man, you join his family in New Jersey every Christmas as well, and graduations, christenings, birthdays, Thanksgivings. Once, you even went to mass, lapsed Catholics though you both were, with his parents and your visiting mother who were not. It was a good life, a wonderful life. The movies of your childhood and his soundtracked your America. Because you are American, became American long before this man in your life, except that he *is* the America you ought to have married because it was the one you imagined as a child in Hong Kong. Well, perhaps not quite. Your invisible America was greener, cleaner, larger than a railroad flat in Manhattan. You would have a piano, because there always was one in your life. The American you did marry was a music man so there was a piano, and a drum set, and guitars, and an electronic keyboard, and amplifiers, sound makers a-plenty. Until it all went silent. Marriages do that, go silent I mean, while *the music box plays on*. But that's another story of the *backward view*, as the past articulates in Chinese.

Was Hoagy Carmichael your America? By now you can't be sure because his music is mashed up with the soundtracks of memory. Didn't you always *know* 'Stardust' or 'Lazy River' or 'Two Sleepy People' or, yes! 'Heart & Soul' which every ivory tickler knows from even her tiny person time? Hadn't you seen him in the old Black & Whites late at night, gabbing with those Yankee voices you didn't entirely understand from a world glimpsed in the pages of *Life*? Or is this all just imagination because it's winter on the South Island and you're living with this man who can recite lines from *Rear Window*, *Casablanca*, *Cat on a Hot Tin Roof* and more, who identifies Tinseltown and Americana for you, filling in the knowledge gaps?

That's not quite right. You are not exactly living with this man right now. You're at the top of time and he at almost the other end of the zone stretch across the globe that is Time. This was pre-Skype, which is less long ago than it sounds. You cannot 'see' each other and New Zealand Telecom is outrageously expensive. He lives over there, and you live here in this villa with a garden and a green room with a piano that you play for hours.

That winter, 'The Nearness of You' became your song. So did many others from the American Songbook. You tried to have the piano tuned but rural enclaves are seldom visited by tuners. Besides, it sounded good enough for an amateur like you. The music was more than America or him or you. The piano caressed your hands, danced melodies round your head, sang love songs to you.

And then you no longer lived together, because you bought a home, a real home in America, not the playpen of New Zealand. Greener, cleaner and larger than a New York City railroad flat, although still in New York, though not one you knew existed when you imagined the country from Hong Kong in the little person era. You bought a piano, a bad buy you later discover, because this console will not hold its tuning. Regret passed soon enough. Nights and days of hand holding and dancing. Consolation in your large and green space up north, where the piano was your constant companion.

You envied your ex-husband's guitar portability, and considered learning a woodwind, even stopped to examine a clarinet once in a second-hand store. But the piano! You can lean into its body, stroke its keys, rise and fall to the rhythms of the pedal. Are you being faithful to the man in your life given this promiscuous flirtation with not one, but two pianos? Oh, his stuff is up north (including a bicycle), and your stuff is in the city. You live together; your stuff is in each other's homes. You both embrace George Carlin's monologue on 'Stuff', laugh, even though you've never watched it together. You even get mail in New York City, as you do up north, as you do in New Zealand.

So what is this silence into which you write, into which you stare at a close-up of silent keys? This piano sits in an abandoned space, which, like all abandoned spaces, holds a strange allure. They worry the memory, imprint themselves on your very self once you've left them behind. Is it spaces or pianos you leave behind?

The South Island piano is a light-coloured wood, like oak, and its action recalls a piano you used to play in another time, another space, on a dead end street in New England. You sold that one and got a better one that thrummed through you, resonant. And then you sold that one to live for a spell in Cincinnati where a swimming pool was the most desirable feature. It would be a long time before another upright entered your life and when it did, the musician was abandoned, along with his guitars and amplifiers and drum set and the electric keyboard in Singapore on which you practised 'La Vie En Rose', a song he never heard you play.

These are years, mind you, we're discussing here. Decades. These are not the passing flirtations of youth.

You time-trip into today and find you cannot abandon Mother. She is old. She cannot remember. Instead, you abandon the hopeless piano that will not hold its tuning in northern New York. You rent out the South Island crib to strangers whom you never meet. You do all this in order to come 'home' to stay till Mother is silenced for ever. The pianos sit silent.

And now you really do not live with the man in your life in the upside-down time zone and you sleep when he wakes and wake when he sleeps.

For a brief while, when abandonment was less certain, you spent half a year in the middle of America in a rented space. The house was large and historic and in the garage was an abandoned piano, wedged amid the detritus of a household. You opened its lid, tickled it awake, but it was a little far gone. Besides, it was heavy and immoveable and this was the dead of winter. But desire smouldered.

At the music store you tested the weighted keys of an electric keyboard and brought that to your space.

This was when you still lived in almost the same time zone with the man in your life. He was to visit the cornfields of Iowa where you were settled for a brief spell but Manhattan held him in bondage. He never saw middle America after all, and still has not, this American lover of yours. You write about being American to articulate what it is you have become.

At the University of Iowa, the library had a section of music scores. You found the Hoagy song book and there, in it, the anthem for the next years of your life (although you did not know it then). When your brother the composer visited, you played it for him. *Listen*, you said, *I think this was Hoagy's heart*. Your brother the church musician does not always share your taste in music, but this time, he asked for a copy of the score for 'Winter Moon' and you made it for him, gladly.

♣

'The American dream,' Carlin said, 'you have to be asleep to believe it.'

In the little person time, you dreamed yourself into an America of desire, to escape the Hong Kong prison into which you were born, where your voice felt continually silenced.

Now, back in this birth city you abandoned to be with the man in your life, you install not one, but two electronic keyboards. The multiple sound tracks – *vox humana*, every instrument of the big band and orchestra, sound effects – sit beside your bed. The weighted keys sit in your writing space. The simulation that feels almost like a real piano switches on, comes alive, holds your hand, caresses your heart.

The man in your life is on Skype when schedules mesh.

And you? You listen to Hoagy sing 'Winter Moon'. You play his songs. You sing the lines to his chord changes.

The other night at a dinner, someone actually sang 'The Sound of Silence' and the audience sang along. Time journeys, nostalgia for youth. And you. You wait, like a winter moon, for summer's return.

WRITER'S NOTE

'Winter Moon' is the title of a song by Hoagy Carmichael and Harold Adamson. Carmichael (1899-1981) was an American composer who is best-known for songs such as 'Stardust', 'Heart & Soul', 'The Nearness of You' and 'Georgia on My Mind'.

WRITERS

RICHARD BEARD has published five novels including *X 20 A Novel of (not) Smoking* (1996), *Damascus* (1999), which was a *New York Times* Notable Book of the Year, *Dry Bones* (2004) and *Lazarus is Dead* (2011). In 2008 he was shortlisted for the BBC National Short Story Award and in 2010 longlisted for the *Sunday Times* EFG Private Bank Short Story Award. He is Director of the National Academy of Writing in London.

ANDREW BLACKMAN's debut novel *On the Holloway Road* (Legend Press, 2009) won the Luke Bitmead Writer's Bursary and was shortlisted for the Dundee International Book Prize. Blackman spent six years in New York, where he worked as a staff reporter for the *Wall Street Journal* and wrote for newspapers and magazines across America. He now lives in London. *A Virtual Love*, a novel on identity in the age of social networking will be published in 2013.

SJ BUTLER is a freelance writer who lives in East Sussex. Her first short story, 'The Swimmer', was published in *The Warwick Review* and then selected for *Best British Short Stories 2011* (Salt Publishing, 2011). She has since had stories published in *Paraxis*, *Litro* and *Untitled*. She blogs at www.underthebookshelf.blogspot.com

MYRIAM FREY is a Swiss writer, translator and illustrator. A trained architect, she is happy to have rediscovered the creative path she has strayed from many years ago. Her short stories have appeared in *Ambit* and at Paraxis.org. Myriam lives in Olten, Switzerland, with her husband and two children. www.myriamfrey.ch

SL GREY is a collaboration between South African writers Sarah Lotz and Louis Greenberg. Their first novel, *The Mall*, was published in 2011 and was followed by *The Ward* in 2012. They blog at http://slgrey.bookslive.co.za.

TANIA HERSHMAN's first book, *The White Road and Other Stories* (Salt, 2008), was commended in the 2009 Orange Award for New Writers, and included in *New Scientist*'s Best Books of 2008. Her collection of short stories *My Mother Was an Upright Piano: Fictions* was published in 2012 (Tangent Books). Her stories have been widely published and broadcast. She is writer-in-residence in Bristol University's Science Faculty. www.taniahershman.com

JAMES HIGGERSON is a writer, music reviewer and urban health researcher from Manchester. His debut novel, *The Almost Lizard*, will be published in Spring 2013 by Legend Press. A selection of his fiction, reviews and rantings are at www.jameshiggerson.com.

JUSTIN HILL is the author of five books and winner of the Geoffrey Faber Memorial Prize, the Betty Trask and Somerset Maugham Awards, as well as being shortlisted and nominated for a host of other awards, including the Booker. *The Drink and Dream Teahouse* was banned in China and picked by the *Washington Post* as one of the best novels of 2001. *Shieldwall*, is the first of a series of books about England's epic tale: 1066 and the Norman Conquest. His books have been translated into 15 languages. www.justinhillauthor.com

NICHOLAS HOGG was nominated for the IMPAC prize for his debut novel *Show Me the Sky*. Winner of the New Writing Ventures Award and of prizes in the Willesden Herald, Bridport and Raymond Carver competitions, his work has also been broadcast by the BBC. He co-created the Photo Stories project – an experiment in writing, photography and design – exhibited at Saatchi & Saatchi and Foyles. His second novel, *The Hummingbird and the Bear*, was published in 2011. www.nicholashogg.com

AVA HOMA is a Kurdish-Canadian writer and academic. Her collection of short stories, *Echoes from the Other Land* was nominated for the 2011 Frank O'Connor International Short Story Award. Ava's writings have appeared in various journals including the *Toronto Quarterly*, *Windsor Review*, and the *Kurdistan Tribune*. She's working on a novel and teaches Creative Writing and English in George Brown College, Toronto, Canada.

AAMER HUSSEIN was born in Karachi in 1955 and moved to London in 1970. His first story appeared in 1987. His stories have since been widely anthologised and translated into Italian, French, Arabic and Japanese. He has published five collections of short fiction, including *Insomnia* (2007), and two novels, *Another Gulmohar Tree* (2009) and *The Cloud Messenger* (2011). He has recently contributed stories to *Granta*, *New Statesman*, *Moth*, *Siecle 21* and *The Critical Muslim*.

NINA KILLHAM is the author of three novels: *How to Cook a Tart*, *Mounting Desire* and *Believe Me*. She also writes short stories and screenplays. She is an American married to an Australian and lives with her two tri-national children in Crouch End, north London.

DEBORAH KLAASSEN (1984) is a Dutch, London-based blogger, essayist, philosopher, copywriter and the author of the horror novel *Bek dicht en dooreten!* (Shut Up and Eat!). She likes to play the violin and misses going to university. Her London blog is at debbiedoeslondon. blogspot.com.

SARAH LADIPO MANYIKA was raised in Nigeria and has lived in Kenya, France and England. Her debut novel, *In Dependence*, was published by Legend Press (2008). She currently lives in California, where she teaches at San Francisco State University and is working on her second novel.

CLAIRE MASSEY is a writer and editor. Her short stories have been published online and in print in various magazines and anthologies including *The Best British Short Stories 2011, Patricide* and *A cappella Zoo*. Two of her stories have recently been published as chapbooks by Nightjar Press. She lives in Lancashire with her two young sons and keeps a blog called Gathering Scraps.

JAN VAN MERSBERGEN, born 1971, stands at the forefront of new Dutch writing. He has written six novels, his latest, *Naar de overkant van de nacht*, was published in October 2011. His novel *Morgen zijn we in Pamplona* was translated into English in 2010 (*Tomorrow Pamplona*, Peirene Press). 'Pa-dang' is his first English-language story.

BARBARA MHANGAMI-RUWENDE is from Zimbabwe. She worked in Germany and studied at the University of Glasgow before moving to the US in 1997, where she attended the Johns Hopkins Bloomberg School of Public Health and Walden University. She lives in Ann Arbour, Michigan, with her husband and four daughters. She is currently working on a short story collection and a novel.

JAMES MILLER was born in London in 1976 and educated at Oxford University, University College London and King's College London. He is the author of the acclaimed literary thrillers *Lost Boys* (Little, Brown, 2008) and *Sunshine State* (Little, Brown, 2010). He currently teaches creative writing and English literature at Kingston University. www.jamesmillerauthor.com

MARK PIGGOTT is from London. His first two novels, *Fire Horses* and *Out of Office*, were published by Legend Press, and he has now completed a third, *emptiness*. His short stories have been published in a wide range of magazines and anthologies including *3:AM, Pulp Books* and *Prole*, and he is a regular contributor to national newspapers including the *Times*. www.markpiggott.com

MARY RECHNER is from Oregon. Her stories have appeared in the *New England Review*, *Kenyon Review*, *Washington Square*, *Propeller Quarterly* and *Oregon Literary Review*. Her criticism and essays have appeared in *The Believer* and *The Oregonian*. Her story collection, *Nine Simple Patterns for Complicated Women*, was published in 2010 by Propeller Books.

DAVID ROSE was born in 1949 and lives in Middlesex. He was forty when his debut story was published in the *Literary Review*. He has since had around three dozen stories published in literary magazines and anthologies, as well as a mini-collection, *Stripe*, and a chapbook, *Being A Greek* (both published by Black Bile Press of Ottawa). His first novel, *Vault*, was published in 2011 (Salt Publishing).

NICHOLAS ROYLE is the author of a short story collection, two novellas and six novels. He has edited fifteen anthologies including *Darklands*, *Murmurations: An Anthology of Uncanny Stories About Birds* and *The Best British Short Stories 2012*. A senior lecturer in creative writing at Manchester Metropolitan University, he also runs Nightjar Press, publishing original short stories as signed, limited-edition chapbooks. His next novel, *First Novel*, is due to be published by Jonathan Cape in 2013.

PREETA SAMARASAN grew up in Malaysia. Her first novel, *Evening is The Whole Day*, has been translated into fourteen languages and was shortlisted for the Commonwealth First Book Award. One of her short stories won a 2010 PEN/O. Henry Prize in the US. She currently lives in France, where she is working on her second novel.

JAN WOOLF is a London-based writer and reviewer. She has spent many years as a special needs teacher and political activist. Her time as a film censor provided material for her first play *Porn Crackers* produced at the Hackney Empire in 2009 – where she held the first Harold Pinter writers' residency. Her collection of short stories, *Fugues on a Funny Bone*, is published by muswell-press.co.uk.

EVIE WYLD's first novel, *After the Fire, a Still Small Voice* (Jonathan Cape, 2009) won the John Llewllyn Rhys Prize and a Betty Trask Award. She was shortlisted for the Orange Prize for New Writers and listed by the *Culture Show* as one of their Best New British Writers, as well as being shortlisted for the IMPAC Award. Her second novel, *All the Birds, Singing*, is due to be published in 2013.

XU XI is a Chinese-Indonesian native of Hong Kong and author of nine books of fiction and essays, most recently, *Access: Thirteen Tales* (2011) and the novel *Habit of a Foreign Sky* (2010), shortlisted for the inaugural Man Asian Literary Prize. She is Writer-in-Residence at the Department of English, City University of Hong Kong, where she established and directs the world's first low-residency MFA in creative writing that focuses on Asia. www.xuxiwriter.com

PHOTOGRAPHER

ROELOF BAKKER is a London-based artist-photographer originally from the Netherlands. The photographs in this book are from *Still*, a photographic and video exploration of vacated interior spaces at Hornsey Town Hall, north London – a municipal heritage-listed building not in public use since the 1980s. An exhibition of photographs and the accompanying video was held at Hornsey Town Hall in November 2010. Most of the photographs from *Still* were recorded on square-format negative film.

A series of photographs from *Still* won first prize (Gold) at the London Photographic Association Still Life 5 competition (June 2011). Bakker's postcard diary exhibition *365 Days* was *Time Out* Arts Critics' Choice (April 2006). His videowork *Wanderlust* (30mins, 2011) has been shown in London, Cheltenham and Roanoke, Virginia, USA. A series of photographs exploring human impact on sports equipment, *Leap*, was exhibited in 2012 as part of the London 2012 Cultural Olympiad at Bruce Castle Museum in Tottenham, north London. www.rbakker.com

LIST OF PHOTOGRAPHS

Below are the titles of the photographs featured in this book in order
of appearance. Titles refer to the names of the spaces as these appear
on the original architectural drawings of 1935.

ACKNOWLEDGEMENTS

Roelof Bakker would like to thank all contributing writers for making *Still* a truly collaborative literary art book.

Many thanks to Andrew Blackman and Nicholas Royle for their support, advice and author suggestions; a special thank-you to Nicholas Royle and Ros Sales for their meticulous copy-editing and many thanks to Nicholas Hogg for exhibition advice.

Special thanks to Ruth Boswell and Jan Woolf at Muswell Press; Clare Hey at Shortfire Press; Meike Ziervogel at Peirene Press; Lauren Parsons at Legend. Also many thanks to Ian Brinley, Steve Amor and Lorraine Sparkes at Haringey Council; and to Robert Bevan, Martin Crawley, David Rice and Paul Savage.

This book is dedicated to the memory of Nigel Jackson.

www.neg-press.com